THE GATE 2

13 TALES OF ISOLATION AND DESPAIR

EDITED BY ROBERT J. DUPERRE

ILLUSTRATED BY JESSE DAVID YOUNG

PRESENTED BY

T.R.O. PUBLISHING

THE GATE 2: 13 TALES OF ISOLATION AND DESPAIR

The stories within this book are works of fiction. Resemblance to any person, living or dead, actual circumstances or events, are purely incidental.

TABLE OF CONTENTS

THE GATE 2: 13 TALES OF ISOLATION AND DESPAIR

INTRODUCTION

When I was young, I loved being alone. I would sit in my room for hours, writing stories or drawing comic books, oblivious to the outside world. I cherished those solitary moments, so much so that when my parents punished me I took it as a blessing. There was so much joy to be had in isolation, so many places my young mind could go if there weren't outside influences to distract me.

Then I grew up.

After being married and having a family, I came to realize that my secluded personal time was a fleeting ideal. I longed for it, wishing, just wishing, that somehow I'd be left alone for an hour, a day, a week. It wasn't until my subsequent divorce, when I had more lonely nights to wallow in depression than I could have wished for, that I realized how much of a folly my previous desire for solitude had been.

Hence I come to the dual themes of this anthology: isolation and despair. They are states of being seemingly unique to the human condition, and after going through my own dark time experiencing just how miserable life can be when you're cut off from your previous existence, it has fascinated me. Many of the stories I've written over the years have dealt with these very same premises, and it has long been my desire to see how other writers deal with them in their own work.

With that in mind, I was lucky enough to have twelve fantastic authors contribute to this anthology. I'm extremely proud of everything they've provided me. These are dark tales, some supernatural, some not, some slice-of-life, some true horror. This being a themed collection, I can honestly say that each and every author put their all into what they presented me, and created something great.

David Dalglish, Mercedes M. Yardley, David McAfee, and Daniel Pyle, each of whom had stories in the first book, have returned for more. The new additions are all people whose works I've reviewed or read and thoroughly enjoyed. There are independent authors Dawn McCullough-White, J.L. Bryan, Joel Arnold, Michael Crane, and D.P. Prior. Each of these individuals has created wonderful stories that are among the best I've read. Then there is my old friend Benjamin X. Wretlind, who I first met more than ten years ago when we were both members of the old Writer's BBS and is one of the most creative and inventive authors around. Added to the mix is my pseudo-boss K. Allen Wood, owner and lead editor of Shock Totem Magazine, a publication I can proudly say my reviews appear within. And yes, he's a very talented writer in his own right, one who's been selfless enough to pony up his own cash to give unknown authors a fantastic outlet for their work, which obviously cuts down on the time he has to create his own.

And finally we have Steven Pirie, another old friend from the BBS days who also happens to be, in my personal opinion, the greatest writer of this generation. He's hilarious and poignant, and his two published novels, *Digging Up Donald* and *Burying Brian*, are number one and two, respectively, on my list of all-time favorite books. And I mean that. To have him provide a story to this collection brings a huge smile to my face.

One final note: You will notice the subtitle of this collection states there are thirteen stories within, but I have added two bonus stories, tales written by myself that were published last year in different anthologies, because their subject matter fits beautifully with the theme. In other words, you get fifteen stories for the price of thirteen. Aren't we generous?

So turn the page, and get lost in the worlds these wonderful creators have conceived.

Sincerely,
RJD

THE GATEKEEPER SEES ALL...

"It's so cold."

Johnny Pazarelli, the Gatekeeper, floats through the emptiness of time and space, particles of his being stretching out, growing larger, more substantial, holding back the warping walls of reality. Images flash through his mind, but he can only watch, not interact. A sinking sensation fills his ethereal stomach. Somewhere back in the real world, his physical body wretches.

"What is wrong?" asks the voice of Albert Mueller, his guide.

"I feel loneliness. I feel sadness."

Albert laughs, and the sound vibrates through the cosmos.

"You are not alone in those emotions," he says. "Not at all. And for some, if they are lucky, there is light at the end of that tunnel...though I would not count on it. Open your eyes, Mr. Pazarelli, and see for yourself."

Johnny does.

PLASTIC

by J.L. Bryan

Jeremy stood at the front doors of the Hazelpointe Meadows shopping mall in Hazelpointe, Ohio. The security mesh was down, blocking the row of still-fully-intact sliding glass doors. This was a good sign. All signs pointed to "yes," as the Magic Eight-ball would say.

Hazelpointe itself had looked like a good prospect to him, a Rust Belt boom town with a dwindling population, small enough to stay off the radar of roving marauders, large enough that people would have fled from it when The Cough hit it big and everyone was desperate to avoid population centers.

Jeremy found the name of the mall amusing, too. Hazelpointe Meadows—a boxy, ugly concrete and glass shell, in the center of a sea of blacktop, fronted by an archipelago of restaurants like Red Lobster and Hooters facing the six-lane road. There wasn't a meadow in sight. Nor any hazel.

He shrugged the hiking pack off his shoulders and set it on the wide concrete step beside him, on top of yellowed cigarette butts and fossilized blobs of chewing gum. He opened a side pocket and lifted out a soft purple bag stitched with the Crown Royal logo, and then he opened the drawstring. The Magic Eight-ball was inside, cushioned by thick wads of tissue paper.

Jeremy lifted it out.

"What do you think, Eight-ball?" he asked. "Should we camp here tonight?"

He gave it a shake.

Ghostly letters floated up from the dark blue fluid inside: "Reply hazy, try again."

"Feeling cranky today?" Jeremy shook it again. The Magic Eight-ball was his priest, attorney, and grief counselor. In the months he'd been wandering the American hellscape alone, Jeremy had felt overwhelmed by all the decisions he faced at every moment, the endless uncertainty. There was no one to help him make any choices. Eight-ball kept him moving, and kept him mostly sane.

"Ask again later," Eight-ball now advised.

9

"Come on!" Jeremy shook it harder now. "Should we stay here or not?"

"My reply is no," Eight-ball finally answered.

"You're crazy, Eight-ball." Jeremy glanced around. The place looked secure, untouched since the Cough. From the mammoth marquee sign out front, he knew there was a Freddy Fisherman's, a megastore supplying hikers, campers, and hunters as well as fishermen. All the things he needed would be there.

Jeremy carefully returned Eight-ball to the pouch, then opened the main pocket of his backpack and took out a few tools. Within twenty minutes, he'd cut through the security mesh and smashed one of the doors. He stepped inside the mall.

Though it was June, and thick afternoon sun flooded in from the skylights overhead, the cavernous indoor mall felt chilly. That meant a working thermostat and HVAC system...and that meant electricity. With electrical lines falling and unmanned power plants breaking down everywhere, most places no longer had any power. He relished the rare kiss of cold air on his skin.

He strolled through the central corridor. The mall was still decorated for Christmas. Stockings and wreaths hung on the storefronts and the second-story banister overhead. He passed Santa's elevated red throne, surrounded by heaps of cotton-puff snow.

He checked the mall directory, then headed for Freddy Fisherman's.

It looked like the mall had been locked down before being abandoned, and that was a good thing. When raiding houses, he usually had to start by dragging the rotten corpses of the former inhabitants out to the back yard, then opening a few windows to wash out the stench of disease and death while he picked through their belongings.

The Cough had taken nearly everyone. Jeremy himself had sat with his mother while the infection consumed her over the course of two weeks. She'd coughed up dark phlegm, and then blood, and finally her frothy, liquified stomach lining. Jeremy's immunity to the Cough must have come from his father, who had died of a heart attack twelve years ago.

At thirty-four, Jeremy had still lived in his childhood bedroom at his mother's house. He'd been an assistant manager at Game

PLASTIC

Stop before the Cough wiped out civilization, taking the video-game market along with it.

He'd left his small hometown in California to look for other survivors, but so far he'd only spotted one rough-looking band of raiders, mostly male, and he'd hidden from them. He took cars and trucks as he needed, and lived mostly on canned food, chocolate bars and bottled soda, whatever he could forage.

Jeremy broke into Freddy Fisherman's and found the camping department. He stuffed his backpack full of protein bars and canned juices before moving on to the gear. The store had tents, camping stoves, generators, and even fuel for the generators.

"Look at all this, Eight-ball," Jeremy said. He lifted Eight-ball from his backpack and held it up as if it were a giant eyeball, like the dripping eye shared by the blind witches from *Clash of the Titans*. "You were wrong, weren't you? When you told me not to stop here?"

He gave Eight-ball a shake.

"Signs point to yes," Eight-ball replied.

"Heck yeah they do," Jeremy said. "You should listen to me more often."

Jeremy filled a shopping cart with generators, lanterns, a couple of stoves, and fuel, then wheeled all of it out to his camper-top truck in the parking lot. By the time he left the mall, he thought the truck would be groaning under the weight of his booty.

After loading his supplies, Jeremy took a break on a bench inside the mall. He was tired, but not yet sleepy. The mall seemed like a safe, well-provisioned place to spend the night—in fact, after the barns and attics he'd slept in lately, it was practically a five-star hotel.

He stood up, stretched, and started exploring. At Radio Shack, he blasted the Rolling Stones over multiple stereos. Then he switched over to Dean Martin, one of his mother's favorites. Later, he could come back and watch a Blu-ray on a plasma screen or three. Plenty of entertainment here.

He reached the Macy's at one end of the mall. The multi-level department store struck him as a kind of vast communal mansion. The bedding department had a number of complete bedroom set-ups, with matching furniture. After that there were rows of living rooms, dining rooms, offices. A large number of people could have eaten at the tables, retired to the sofas, and slept in the beds. Jeremy thought about Goldilocks and the Three Bears.

That night he slept in a California King bed at Macy's.

Over the next few weeks Jeremy kept planning to leave and kept failing to do it. He had every material comfort at hand. He knew he would never make contact with any other people if he stayed cocooned inside the mall—but then, there was no guarantee that any people he found out in the world would treat him well. The mall was a safe place to be.

On the last day of his usual routine, Jeremy woke, stretched, and made up his bed. He greeted the mannequins as he passed them. He had names for those he saw regularly. The man with the fishing hat and matching pole was Gramps; the guy with the sunglasses perched on top of his head and the sweater arms draped around his neck was Skipster; the snooty women in tennis outfits were Marla and Ivana.

Jeremy brewed himself some stale coffee at Seattle's Best and read a magazine. Every day he read the final issue of a different newspaper or magazine. Today it was the final issue of *Time*, and the cover story was, naturally, about The Cough. "Who will cure The Cough?" the headline asked.

"Nobody," Jeremy said. He read the story anyway, about universities, hospitals, and the CDC working day and night to fight the disease. The tone of the article was cautiously optimistic. The article's writer, and every person interviewed in the article, were now dead. Jeremy was pretty certain of that.

After coffee, he took a walk through the mall. He picked a few stores each day to thoroughly inventory, jotting down their merchandise on a yellow legal pad. Partly, this was so he wouldn't leave without missing something he could use, but mostly it just felt productive and cut the boredom.

As he passed the Hot Topic, he slowed his walk and glanced sheepishly at the mannequins in the window. Three women, all dressed in a kind of punk Goth fashion. The one in front had long blond hair and an exceptionally beautiful face, in his opinion, with dark shadowed eyes and dark purple lipstick. She wore a spiked leather dog collar, skimpy mesh shirt, lacy black miniskirt. Jeremy had already memorized her appearance, down to the purple toenails in her spiked black shoes.

PLASTIC

"Hi, Melissa," Jeremy said. Was he actually blushing? "Hi, Kristen, Catelyn," he said to her two friends. The girls didn't respond to him at all, as if he didn't even exist—which was to say, they treated him exactly the way real women always had.

He continued on, all the way to the Sears at the opposite end of the mall from the Macy's. He was looking at the assortment of power tools when it happened.

The overhead lights blacked out all at once, and the department store fell into darkness. The only illumination was dust-filled sunlight from the row of exterior doors, where metal security mesh sliced the light like prison bars.

Not even the EXIT signs glowed.

Jeremy cursed. This was going to make life less pleasant.

He walked away from the chainsaws, found a shopping cart, and began gathering flashlights and batteries.

Over the next several days—he had long since lost track of time, and didn't know a Friday from a Sunday—Jeremy became gradually convinced that the mannequins watched him from the shadows, maybe even whispered about him behind his back. With the loss of power, it could sometimes be hard to read the mannequins' faces or discern where their eyes were looking. Something weird was definitely happening at the mall.

One night, sitting in his easy chair and reading a paperback by candlelight, he thought he heard laughter. He stood up and searched the Macy's, but he couldn't find anyone. The mannequins watched him with smug, plastic smiles.

A few days after that, he tried carrying on with his morning routine—Gramps told him that the fish were biting well, Skipster was worried about how the extinction of humanity might impact bond futures, Ivana and Marla gossiped about their wild night at the T.G.I. Friday's bar on the mall's first floor.

Strolling through the mall, Jeremy realized he had no excuse to pass by Hot Topic today. He'd already mentally inventoried everything on that end of the mall.

He walked past it anyway, and said good morning to Kristen, Catelyn, and especially Melissa, who just looked back at him with cool, blank eyes. He didn't hear any of them say good morning back, but then again they never did. He wondered whether they talked about him after he passed by each morning.

He walked down the frozen escalator, and then doubled back on the second floor. This meant he had to pass the Abercrombie & Fitch, and he didn't trust the gang of suspiciously cheerful adolescents hanging out in their window. Jeremy hurried past them and on down to King's Jewelry to continue the inventory.

That night, he had a special question for Eight-ball. He didn't want anyone to overhear, so he took Eight-ball to the art gallery, where nobody was around except for a couple of stone lions and a ceramic dalmatian.

"Eight-ball," Jeremy whispered, "Should I ask Melissa on a date?"

"Concentrate and ask again," Eight-ball answered.

"What's there to concentrate on?" he asked. "She's the hottest girl in the whole mall, and I think I've seen her looking at me a couple of times. I know she never speaks to me. But maybe she's shy? Is that it, Eight-ball? Melissa's just shy like me, isn't she?"

"Very doubtful," Eight-ball replied.

"You're right, of course she isn't," Jeremy said. "She's too pretty for that. Do you think...Eight-ball, do you think she likes me?"

"Don't count on it," Eight-ball said.

"You're right, I shouldn't count on it. I have to win her over. What if I ask her out to T.G.I. Friday's? We could have a couple of drinks, some peanut butter granola bars...Do you think she'll go along with that, Eight-ball?"

"Without a doubt," Eight-ball assured him.

Jeremy made his move the next day, after dressing in the best clothes he could find—black shirt and black pants, since he knew she liked black, plus some expensive shoes that might impress her. He spritzed on some cologne as he passed through the fragrance department.

He was nervous as he stepped inside Hot Topic and approached the three tough-but-sexy girls in the window. None of them greeted him, or acknowledged him in any way, which made him even more nervous.

"Hi, Melissa," he said to the beautiful blond girl. She didn't respond. He wished her two friends would go away, but they didn't show any sign of budging. "Listen...I know this is unexpected...and I'm just a...but...well, anyway, do you want to go on a dinner with me? A date, I mean? Like, tonight?"

PLASTIC

Melissa just looked at him. Jeremy thought he heard her two friends snickering behind him, but when he looked they were completely quiet again, their faces blank.

"Are you turning me down?" Jeremy asked. She didn't answer. "So, can I pick you up at eight, then?"

Jeremy thought he saw the shadow of a smile about to form on her lips. Her friends giggled again, and when he turned to face them the two goth girls seemed to be giving him a friendlier look.

His heart skipped. He had a date.

They had drinks in a booth at T.G.I. Friday's. Melissa didn't touch her protein bar, but he'd heard that women often didn't eat on first dates. She didn't have much to say, either, but she watched him attentively while he told her about his life before The Cough and the girl he'd had a crush on in high school (Misty Townsend, who ended up marrying Jason Pilcher, the jerk, and together they'd bought the biggest house in Jeremy's mom's neighborhood).

After dinner, they went for a stroll through the forest of artificial ferns at the food court, and on down to the big central water fountain. Jeremy pushed her in a shopping cart so she didn't have to walk. She seemed to want him to handle most of the conversation, and Jeremy struggled for more things to talk about. Fortunately she never yawned, or said anything about ending their date.

When they reached Macy's, Jeremy took a chance and invited her in. While she didn't exactly say "yes" or "no," he thought she had a sly, seductive look on her face.

He showed her around Macy's, and eventually took her to his bed. She didn't resist as he kissed her, laid her down, and slowly undressed her. Then Jeremy took off his clothes and climbed into bed beside her.

"I've never done this before," he whispered.

She didn't seem to mind.

* * *

He felt sure everyone was talking about it the next day. Ivana and Marla wanted all the details, of course, so they could gossip with their friends in Ladies' Professional Wear. Gramps just winked when Jeremy walked by.

15

Melissa, happily, seemed content to stick around over the following days and weeks (Jeremy had lost track of time altogether, except for the steady pulse of day and night, which he only noticed because he had to use electric lanterns or light candles). Melissa never said a word about going back to Hot Topic. Jeremy found her lovemaking a little stiff and unresponsive, but he didn't have much experience with which to compare it.

They went on little trips around the mall. He used a generator to fuel a projector in the multiplex theater, and they made out together in the darkened back row. Melissa wasn't a big walker. She liked for Jeremy to carry her in his arms or roll her around in the cart. As a gift to her, he spray painted her cart black and decorated it with skulls and spikes from the Hot Topic. He thought she liked that, though she never really mentioned it.

When some more time had passed, he took Eight-ball back to the art gallery, and he asked The Question.

"Eight-ball." Jeremy paused to take a deep breath. "Do you think I should ask Melissa to marry me?"

He gave Eight-ball a shake.

"Concentrate and ask again."

"Why do you always say that about her?" Jeremy snapped. "We love each other, Eight-ball. We should get married, shouldn't we?"

"Ask again later," Eight answered.

Jeremy shook his Eight-ball as hard as he could. "What is wrong with you? Are you jealous of her?"

"Don't count on it," Eight-ball replied.

"That's it, isn't it?" Jeremy held Eight-ball in front of his face and stared into the circular window, the iris of Eight-ball's eye. "I'm going to marry her whether you like it or not. I'm only asking one more time: do you think I should marry Melissa? And if you say 'no' I'll smash you against that stupid stone lion over there."

"Better not tell you now," Eight-ball said.

"Should I propose or not?" Jeremy gave Eight-ball a furious shake.

"My sources say no."

"Go to hell!" Jeremy shouted. Following through on his promise, he bashed Eight-ball against the ear of a snarling stone lion. Eight-ball's shell cracked, and blue liquid gushed like blood between Jeremy's fingers. It smelled like alcohol.

PLASTIC

He swung Eight-ball again. Half the shell broke away and thumped to the floor at Jeremy's feet, and blue alcohol splashed his t-shirt, soaking him. A twenty-sided die, Eight-ball's brain, skipped out of the art gallery and rolled across the second-floor walkway. He watched it spin away under the banister and out of sight, and heard it bounce across the food court below.

"I'm making my own choices from now on," Jeremy said, and he flung aside the remaining broken plastic chunk of Eight-ball.

He started to leave, but then he noticed the blue alcohol soaking his hands and shirt. Eight-ball's blood. He couldn't let anyone see him like this, or they'd know he was guilty of murder.

He gathered the broken pieces of Eight-ball and stuffed them back into the Crown Royal bag. Then he stripped off his t-shirt, wiped his hands on it, and tossed it in into one of the large trash bins out on the main walkway, next to a bench.

There was one missing piece: Eight-ball's brain. If somebody found that, there could be questions.

He walked down the escalator to the food court, where he checked everywhere, under chairs and tables, but couldn't find the twenty-sided die. Then he noticed someone was watching him—a clown, standing just outside McDonald's. The clown was smiling and waving at him.

"Oh, hi, Ronald," Jeremy said. "I'm just, um, looking for something."

The clown just smiled at him. Jeremy wondered if he'd seen Eight-ball's brain skip through here, but he certainly wasn't going to ask. Jeremy looked suspicious enough, searching frantically around the food court while shirtless.

"Well, guess I better get going," Jeremy said. The clown watched him depart, still smiling, and didn't say a word. Jeremy didn't trust him.

They had a small service at the Family Bible Christian Bookstore, decorated with artificial flowers from the Hallmark shop, officiated by a priest whose plastic vestments and hollow crucifix came from the costume aisle at the party store. It was a quiet affair, with a lot of silent reflection and hardly any guests, since Eight-ball had so few friends.

Melissa came, which was very nice of her, considering Eight-ball had such a low opinion of Jeremy and Melissa's relationship. It made Jeremy love her all the more.

"I guess I should say a few things," Jeremy said. "Eight-ball was my friend. What he really enjoyed was answering questions. Sometimes his answers were very clear, and sometimes they were kind of vague, but he always had an answer for you." Jeremy's throat clenched up. He felt like a horrible hypocrite, knowing he was the one who'd killed Eight-ball. He didn't know how to handle his guilt and genuine sorrow over the loss of his friend, and of course he could no longer go to Eight-ball for advice.

Jeremy was also the pallbearer. He carried the Eight-ball to one of the fake ferns, lifted it up in its pot, and stuffed Eight-ball into the plastic peat underneath. Eight-ball was buried in the Crown Royal bag he loved so well.

Jeremy noticed an extra guest here at the burial. The clown was watching from McDonald's, waving at Jeremy and giving a macabre smile. Jeremy was pretty sure Ronald knew something, but so far the clown was keeping mum about it.

* * *

Jeremy waited a few days to make sure nobody was talking about the murder. Then he proposed to Melissa at midnight at Yankee Candle, where he'd lit every piece of merchandise in the store to set a romantic scene. The shop smelled like rose, cinnamon, vanilla, jasmine, sandalwood, musk, licorice...Jeremy wanted to gag at the many mingled smells, but he figured women liked that kind of thing.

He dropped to one knee and presented her with the biggest diamond ring that had been on display at King's Jewelers.

"Melissa, you make me happier than I ever thought I could be," he said. "Will you marry me?"

She didn't say no. He slipped the ring on her finger.

They were married by the fountain, under the skylights. The fountain pumps no longer functioned, and the water had gone stagnant, but Jeremy had covered the water with a layer of plastic flowers and floating candles.

Guests came from as far away as Sears. Melissa's old friends wore leather bridesmaids' dresses from Hot Topic. Gramps gave away the bride. Skipster was Jeremy's best man. Jeremy didn't even like Skipster that much, but he didn't have many friends, and

PLASTIC

Skipster hadn't expressed any problem with the idea when Jeremy asked him.

Jeremy wore a black coat with tails from Tuxedo Junction. The priest who had officiated the funeral conducted the service.

Melissa came down the aisle in a white cart festooned with white bunting and more plastic flowers. She was veiled inside her wedding dress, her long lacy train dragging the floor behind her.

When Jeremy finally lifted her veil and kissed her, he thought he heard Marla and Ivana crying in the audience.

They had their reception at T.G.I. Friday's – not only had it been the site of their first date, it was the only place in the mall that served booze.

They honeymooned at the Sears swimwear department, where a photographic mural of a beautiful tropical beach covered the wall from floor to ceiling. Suntanned young people modeling assorted brands of beachwear played volleyball in front of it. To one side there was a tiki hut offering racks of sunglasses. Jeremy and his bride lay on a blanket that evening, watching the sunset through the glass outer doors of Sears.

On subsequent nights he took her to the Sears bedding department. Along the way they passed the menswear department, and Jeremy felt jealous when he noticed the men in their business suits blatantly ogling Melissa in her bikini.

Then the honeymoon was over, and they returned home to Macy's.

"I love you Melissa," he said as they lay together on their first night home. He was spooning her, with his face buried in her long blond hair. She didn't answer him. She must have already been asleep.

For a number of days he felt like she was keeping her distance from him. He suspected there was something she wasn't saying. An unspoken tension began to grow between them.

Then Jeremy figured it out: Melissa was pregnant, but she just didn't know how to tell him.

Then they were happy again, shopping at Big Baby Junction for cribs and bottles. He couldn't believe how quickly her pregnancy progressed. One day she appeared as she always had, ever since the first time he saw her in the window. The next day it looked like someone had shoved a basketball under her maternity dress, and possibly anchored it there with duct tape.

After much anticipation, the big day arrived. It was a difficult delivery—Jeremy had to break her basketball himself with a pen knife to get the air flowing out. In the end, though, it was a beautiful day. Jeremy wheeled their children in from the Gap Kids store. They'd had a boy and a girl, fraternal twins, both of them cute and smiley.

They named the twins Sammy and Suzy. Sammy got a race-car bed, while Suzy got a princess bed with a frilly canopy. They all lived happily at Macy's.

Having children changed Melissa. She moved on from her spiked collars and leather pants to prim blouses and ankle-length skirts, just like Jeremy's mother used to wear. She took the kids down the escalator to Sylvan Learning Center each morning. On Sundays Melissa made the whole family attend church at Family Bible, where they listened to preachers via audiobook. Jeremy's mother would have liked that too, knowing her grandchildren were getting a good Christian education.

Jeremy sometimes took Sammy over to the sporting goods store and tried to show him how to shoot basketball, but Sammy was a shy, inactive kid. For that matter, Suzy was as much of a wallflower as her mother. Jeremy couldn't believe that he had turned out to be the talkative, outgoing one in the family.

In the summer they packed their kids and their luggage into the family shopping cart and made the long trip to the Sears swimwear department for a beach vacation.

As they lay on their beach towels, Jeremy looked over his family. While he cared about them, he felt like he wasn't really connecting with them anymore. They hardly spoke a word to him, and they never seemed to listen. More and more, they just stared right through him, blankly, whenever he tried to strike up a conversation.

He found himself looking at the tan girls playing volleyball in their bikinis. Melissa didn't wear bikinis anymore, just a dark one-piece with a prim swimming skirt, and Jeremy could sense her disdain for the flirty young things at the beach.

Jeremy didn't feel disdain, though. His eye kept wandering to one of the bikini girls, one with a very dark and exotic skin tone, her hair luxurious and brown. She wore a bikini with a sort of tie-dyed flower pattern.

PLASTIC

Sometimes Jeremy could feel her watching the back of his head. Once or twice he was pretty sure he'd caught her looking at him. And maybe smiling, or just about to do so.

On the sixth day of their vacation, Jeremy found himself staring at the dark beauty again. He glanced over at his wife and kids, stretched out on their beach blankets. None of them were moving. They must have all dozed off.

This was his chance.

He stepped right into the middle of the volleyball game and approached the dark girl in her colorful bikini. Nobody said a word to stop him. He took her by the hand.

He led the girl around behind the tiki hut full of sunglasses, out of sight of his family. The dark-skinned girl must have been feeling eager, because she let him lay her down on the beach blanket and remove her bikini.

Jeremy hurried to get out of his clothes, then he spread her legs and climbed on top of her. He was feeling eager, too, so the whole thing lasted less than two minutes.

When he was done, he rolled off the girl and lay down beside her, but she wasn't looking at him. She was staring straight up at the high ceiling overhead.

"This was a mistake," Jeremy said. "I have to go."

She said nothing, indifferent to him.

Jeremy returned to his family and lay down beside his wife.

"Nice day, isn't it, Melissa?" he asked.

But she didn't have a word to say to him, then or ever again. The kids gave him the silent treatment, too.

When they returned home, Melissa lay rigid in their bed and showed no interest in being intimate with him. After a couple of nights she moved to another bed. He cried and apologized to her again and again, but she said nothing, her face like a hard plastic mask.

Soon after that, Melissa took the kids and moved into Sears at the far end of the mall. The last time he saw her she was with one of those jerks from the menswear department.

Gramps had no sympathy. Neither did Ivana and Marla, who whispered nasty things about Jeremy when he wasn't around, telling everyone on the north end of the mall what he'd done to Melissa and insinuating he'd done a lot more, like hooking up with various women all over Macy's, which was just malicious gossip. Skip didn't seem to care about Jeremy's suffering, either, but he had never been a true friend. None of them had ever been true friends, Jeremy thought. Eight-ball had been the only one he could really trust, and now Eight-ball was gone.

Jeremy worried that word was getting out about his part in Eight-ball's death. While nobody said anything to his face about it, he thought he could sense an air of suspicion. The clown gave him a lot of strange smiles whenever Jeremy passed the food court.

One night he went to T.G.I. Friday's and drank Seagram's straight from the bottle. He found himself wandering through the mall, drinking and weeping. Everyone came to their windows to watch. The college kids at Old Navy, the sexy ladies at Victoria's Secret—all of them watched him, no doubt whispering to each other about how pathetic and worthless he was, how he'd lost his wife to some wingtipped jerkoff over at Sears.

"Go to hell!" he shouted at one placid, grinning face after another. "All of you go to hell!" The place was getting too small for him, with everybody full of gossip and judgment, everybody up in his business.

He found his way out to the parking lot. Jeremy managed to climb inside his truck with the camper top, the one he'd loaded with provisions so long ago. He fumbled the key into the ignition and cranked it up.

He would have to press on without Eight-ball to help him. Jeremy swerved his way down the interstate, steering with one hand, sipping gin with the other. He flipped on the radio and listened to the open hiss of dead air for the rest of the night.

J.L. Bryan *studied English literature at the University of Georgia and at Oxford, with a focus on the English Renaissance and the Romantic period. He also studied screenwriting at UCLA. He enjoys remixing elements of paranormal, supernatural, fantasy, horror and science fiction into new kinds of stories.*

He is the author of The Paranormals *series (*Jenny Pox*,* Tommy Nightmare*, and* Alexander Death*) and other books.* Fairy Metal Thunder *is the first book in his new* Songs of Magic *series. He lives in Atlanta with his wife Christina, his baby son John, and some dogs and cats.*

Website: www.jlbryanbooks.com Twitter: @jlbryanbooks

PLASTIC

THE INDIAN ROPE TRICK

by D.P. Prior

Mum was thump, thump, thumping on the door. It was raining cats and dogs out there. The rat-tat-tat on the windows made the sound of a gazillion BB guns shooting the glass. Thunder cracked and rolled away like angels dropping coal. Inside, the TV was chattering and Dad was nailing planks across the windows. My breaths were raggedy gasps and my heart was bouncing in my chest. Under it all I could hear the groaning of the zombies, and the screaming and the sirens, and the bang, bang, bang of the policemen's guns. I couldn't help myself. My fingers fumbled with the door chain.

"Don't!" Dad dropped his hammer and shoved me out of the way. He checked the latch to make sure Mum couldn't open the door from the outside, and looked through the peephole.

"It's her," I said. "You have to let her in."

He snarled as he turned and grabbed me by the shoulders.

"It's not. Don't you get it? It's not. Oh, Christ, I'm sorry, Wes. I'm not...I mean...I'm not angry with you. We just can't let her in, is all. She's bit."

"Then make her better."

He pinched the top of his nose and screwed his face up. I thought he was gonna cry.

"I can't, Wes. I fuckin'...I can't."

I ducked under his arm so quick he couldn't stop me.

"Wes—"

I pressed my face up against the door and squinted through the peephole. Mum looked sickly and grey, and there was stuff coming out of her mouth, all foamy and disgusting. Her teeth kept snapping together like she was saying something, but all I could hear was her growling.

"You little..." Dad yanked me back and squeezed my cheeks with one hand so I had to look him in the face. "She ain't speaking,

25

Wes. Don't you see? If it was really her, don't you think she'd be yelling or screaming? She's bit, I tell you."

My face felt like it was on fire. I stared him out, but couldn't think of anything to say. I slapped his hand off me and went to look through the gaps in the planks covering the window. I could see the side of Mum's coat. There were carrier bags on the driveway next to her. Back a little way, there was a policeman all in black with one of them bulletproof jackets. He had a rifle gun pointed at her and was shouting the same thing over and over, only I couldn't make out what it was, what with all the other noise. Something shambled past the window. There was a shot and a spray of red on the glass.

"Get away." Dad's voice cracked, like he was crying. "Get back from the window. You don't want … you don't want them to see you."

Mum hit the door real hard just then, thump after thump after thump. The frame shook and Mum's growls turned into angry screams. All I could do was cover my ears and shut my eyes tight, really, really tight. The policeman called out again, this time from closer by. Mum must've thrown herself against the door, 'cause the frame split. Thunder rolled, rain pattered, things moaned, the TV chattered. Someone else shouted, "The head, you tosser!" and there was a deafening bang. I screamed and fell to my knees, trying to breathe. Trying, trying to breathe. I felt Dad's arms around me; heard his sobbing; felt his warm tears on my neck.

"It weren't her," he said through sniffs. "She was already gone, Wes. It weren't her."

He didn't try to hold me back when I stood and looked through the peephole. It was smeared with blood and I couldn't see out.

"Wes…"

"I might be nine, Dad, but I'm not stupid. Got it?"

I pushed past him and headed through the lounge into the kitchen. I tried the back door. It was locked. I could see out into the conservatory through the kitchen window. I knew that was locked, too. We'd checked it earlier, after bringing the planks in from the shed. I heard Dad behind me as I took the key out of the lock.

"What're you doing?" he asked.

"They break the window, they might reach in and turn the key," I said.

He nodded at me. "Too clever for your own good, Wes. Good boy. Should be safe now. Front's all boarded up and there's no sign of them out back."

"We need to barricade the doors," I said. "You know, with chairs and stuff."

"I'm on it," Dad said, going back to the lounge and upturning an armchair.

"*... still no official word on where it came from,*" a reporter was saying on TV. He'd been saying the same thing for hours, and they kept showing a clip of zombies lumbering after a cameraman before they cut to the studio where they asked a bunch of stupid people the same stupid questions and got the same stupid answers. While Dad dragged the chair to the front door, I watched another scene of blue-grey zombies walking all stiff and creepy-like along a London high street. People were screaming and running from them. Then there was a shot of pigs and birds and it was back to the studio.

"Professor Worsley," Will Turner was saying. "We've had dozens of emails asking whether the virus—that is what it is, isn't it?"

"Possibly," said a little round man with a silly beard and glasses. "It's still early days. It could be a bacillus; it could be a freak manifestation of a latent mutation; it could be terrorists. No one knows."

"But do we know if it's spread by animals?" Siobhan Smith asked.

"It could well be." Professor Worsley took off his glasses and rubbed them on his jacket. "But it might not be, as well."

"*Richard Dawkins said it was an act of God,*" Will said.

Worsley huffed at that and put his glasses back on.

"Professor Dawkins was being ironic."

"What do you say to the people who claim it started in a Verusia Labs facility? Do you think it's fair to blame Dr Otto Bligh—"

I switched the TV off.

"What's 'ironic', Dad?"

"Haven't the foggiest," he said, walking into the lounge and looking like he'd forgotten what he was doing, same as Granddad John used to.

"The back," I said with a tut.

"Oh, yeah, right." Dad dragged the other armchair through to the kitchen.

"Fuck!" he yelled, dropping the chair as the cat flap banged shut and Watson hissed. His fur was standing on end like he'd seen a ghost, and his eyes were all white and milky. Dad let out a sigh and bent to stroke him.

"You scared the crap out of me, kitty-cat," he said. "Ow!" He snatched his hand away and covered it with his other hand. "Fuck," he swore again. "Shit. That really hurt."

Blood was seeping between his fingers and pooling on the floor. He grabbed a tea towel to wrap around the bite, but Watson hissed again and pounced. Dad fell backward into the armchair and the cat was on top of him, biting and scratching.

"Get him off me!" Dad cried, thrashing about with his arms and legs. "Wes, get him off!"

I half screamed, half cried as I grabbed a bottle of wine from the rack and clubbed Watson with it. He turned and snarled at me and I hit him again, right in the face. Blood sprayed onto the cabinets, and Watson flopped to the floor. Dad pushed himself out of the armchair and crunched his foot down on Watson's head and kept it there until he stopped moving.

I put my hand to my throat as sickness burned its way up my windpipe.

"Go upstairs!" Dad shouted.

His face was all scratched up, and his neck and arms were bleeding.

"But he's dead." I looked down at the cat's splattered head and dry heaved.

"Now!" Dad yelled, and shoved me back into the lounge.

I stumbled at first, but then turned and ran upstairs. He followed me, and he had that look about him you didn't want to argue with. When we reached the landing, he fetched a chair from his room to stand on. He reached up and unbolted the trapdoor to the attic, then pulled the wooden ladder down.

"Up," he said.

I did as I was told while he threw the chair aside.

"Dad—"

"Just go!"

When I reached the top, I looked back and saw him head downstairs.

THE INDIAN ROPE TRICK

"Are you coming?" I called, but there was no answer.

I paused in the opening, straining to listen. Dad was crashing about in the cupboard under the stairs by the sounds of it. When I heard his heavy footfalls returning, I crawled into the attic and lay on my tummy so I could watch. He appeared on the landing with the big hammer he'd used to break up the decking last winter, when it went all rotten and slimy and someone might have slipped on it and broke their neck. When he reached the ladder, he didn't start to climb up like I'd thought, but he took a swing with the hammer and went right through the wood. He swung again and again, cracking and splintering the ladder until the bottom half fell away.

"Dad, please!"

He kept on bash, bash, bashing till there was a pile of broken wood in the middle of the landing. Then he righted the chair and climbed on it.

"Love you, son," he said with tears in his eyes as he started to close the trapdoor. "Stay still and keep real quiet. Everything's gonna be OK."

In that moment I realized what he was doing. Dad, my daddy, always said he'd protect me from everything. He knew what was going to happen. I did, too, only part of me didn't want to believe it. It was like when I kept trying to believe in Father Christmas even after everyone at school said it was just my parents pretending. As the trap shut and he slid the bolt across, I was left in the dark.

The air was dusty and smelled of woodchips. I heard Dad jump down from the chair, then there were more bangs, cracks, and snaps. He was smashing the chair so he couldn't climb up. Making sure I was safe.

I did as he said and kept as still as a statue, not even daring to breathe. I could hear him moving around for a bit, but then there was a loud thud and nothing more. I sat back against something soft and giving. It rustled like a plastic bag. I lay there for a while, my mind all horrid pictures and no thoughts, body shaking so much I had to hold my knees tight to my chest and rock myself to make it stop. I kept seeing Mum's crazy face, those empty eyes like puddles of milk; the dribble running down her chin. I imagined what it must've looked like when her head exploded all over the door. My brain wouldn't stop playing it over and over, as if I'd really seen it. Bang. Splat. Bang. Splat. Bang.

I became aware of the rain crashing against the roof. There was still the odd gunshot, muffled and far off. People occasionally cried out, but the moaning and groaning never went away. I went from only hearing the sound of my breathing to being deafened by the noises from outside. I wanted them to stop. I needed to hear what was happening indoors. I needed to listen out for Dad. I got back on my tummy and pressed my ear to the trapdoor.

"Dad?" I called out in a shaky voice. "Daddy, are you there?"

My heart started flapping about in my ribcage like a bird in a chimney. I sat up and tried to suck in some air, but none came. I squeezed in a tiny breath, then another, and another till I was panting like a dog. As my breaths got faster and faster, my heart sped up, too. I could hear it inside my head, big sloshy whooshes, like when you're underwater. What was happening to me? Was I ill like those people on TV? Had I got Watson's blood on me? Was I gonna turn into one of *them*? I needed to see. Had to see. I tore into a plastic bag, spilling its fluffy contents. I rummaged about, looking for anything that might help me see, but it was useless. They were just teddies. My old toys that Mum had put out of the way. I recognized them all by touch, ran my hands over them, worked out who they were by the feel of their fur, the size of their eyes. *Mr. Penn!* I found Mr. Penn, my old green dog teddy and hugged him tight. I let out a big sigh and felt my eyes tearing up.

"No time for crying, Mister Penn," I said. "We've gotta find some light."

There was a light switch somewhere near the entrance. I'd seen Dad turn it on when we came up here to play treasure hunt once. With Mr. Penn tucked under one arm, I crawled back toward the trapdoor and felt around in the dark. I found the cold brick wall and ran my fingers along its rough surface until I found the switch. I flicked it and felt a moment's panic when nothing happened. But then the two strip-lights in the ceiling started to flicker and hum, like they were grumpy about being woken up. With a ping and a flash that had me blinking, they snapped on, casting a dirty yellow light over the piles and piles of junk that we'd hidden away up here.

Apart from my teddies, it was mostly boring stuff near the entrance—bed linens, pillows, ugly patterned blankets. Stacked baskets ran down each side of a central aisle, all brimming with odds and ends that no one would ever use.

THE INDIAN ROPE TRICK

There was a canvas wardrobe halfway along, bursting with Mum's old clothes she wouldn't throw away. She said they might fit again one day, once she'd lost a bit of weight. I used to think it was a TARDIS when I was little. That all seemed ten thousand million years ago now. Nine was so much older than eight. 'Specially when the world was going mad and the grown-ups couldn't help you anymore. I still felt the tug of the TARDIS, though. Part of me wanted to believe I could squeeze in amongst all those clothes and escape to another planet. Better still, I could travel back in time and tell Mum not to go shopping so she wouldn't get bitten and turn into a zombie. I could tell Dad to tape up the cat flap. Then they'd both still be with me and we could hide away indoors till the police killed all the zombies and told us it was safe to come out. Kids are stupid like that. I started to feel warm and cozy. Everything I daydreamed about was real, right up until I gave the TARDIS a good look and saw it was just make believe. I turned away from it and dropped Mr. Penn. I had to be tough to get out of this. *Ain't got time to be scared*, Dad used to say when I thought there were monsters under the bed. *Too busy trying to sleep. Ain't got time to cry*, he'd say whenever I grazed my knee. *Too busy playing.*

Toward the far end of the attic there was a big fluffy donkey we called Oswald. He was standing guard over the fake Christmas tree, the one we used to bring down to the lounge every year. My tummy twinged when I thought about it. We would have been doing that in a week or so. Now it would just lie there gathering dust.

I made my way along the aisle, careful to keep to the boards so my feet didn't go through the ceiling. Something squeaked and I stopped, holding my breath. There was a rustle of plastic bags, and I turned to stare as a stack of full black bin liners tumbled down. I strained and strained, but couldn't hear anything else above the drumming of the rain on the roof tiles.

My eyes were drawn to something glinting behind where the bin liners had been stacked. I grabbed a plastic sack and heaved it out of the way, and then stepped carefully between the others. The glint disappeared as I drew nearer. When I craned my neck to look back, it was obvious why. The strip-light in the ceiling was now behind me. It must've been reflecting from something. I pressed on into the shadows with one foot on either side of a load of foamy stuff between the beams. I was never allowed to play near the edges of the attic because they hadn't been boarded over. One wrong step and I'd break my bleeding neck. Least that's what Dad always said.

Just thinking of him was like a punch in the guts. I felt all mangled up inside. The tears wanted to come, but I wouldn't let them. Times like this you need to be strong. No one was coming to save me now. I knew that as sure as I knew Mum would never be stepping through the door and telling me to carry the shopping bags. Dad and I would never form our little chain gang so we could put the tins away in the cupboards while Mum fixed the tea. A sniffle escaped, but I ignored it, peering into the darkness until I could make out a shape blacker than the rest. I reached out and my fingers found something cold and hard. It felt like metal. I crouched down and ran both hands over it. It was a box of some sort, with a lid and handles on either side. I took hold of one of the handles and gave it a tug. The box shifted easier than I thought and I fell backward. I threw my hand out behind and struck foam. My heart jumped into my throat and I shut my eyes, waiting to fall through the ceiling. I must've got lucky 'cause nothing happened. After a few raspy breaths, I inched back onto the beams and found the handle again. This time, I took little steps backward as I dragged the box into the light.

It was painted black, but was chipped all over. It looked a thousand years old. Maybe a million. There was a tiny key in the lock, with a ripped brown tag attached to it. *Wesley J. Harding*, it said in swirly joined-up writing. Except for the J., that was my name, but I'd never seen the box before in my life. Then I remembered something Dad had told me when I was really little. I was named after his great, great, great granddad, but my middle name was different. That was Xavier, after this saint Mum liked. Dad once told me he was eaten by cannon-balls. But Wesley J. Harding was real famous in my family. He was in India, they said. In the stories Dad used to tell, he was always doing magic stuff, like rope tricks so he could escape from the evil tiger-men. He could even lie on a bed of nails without getting pricked to death.

I turned the key and lifted the lid. It fell back on its hinges with a loud clang. There was an answering growl from below. It sounded like those things from outside, only it was definitely closer; right underneath me. I closed my eyes to listen better. Someone moaned, and there was a noise like Darth Vader breathing and Dad gargling TCP all rolled into one.

"Daddy?" I said, too softly for him to hear. Then a little louder, "Dadda?"

There was a snarl, then lots of smashing and crashing, like someone was throwing furniture about. There was a heavy thud right beneath the attic, and more moaning and groaning that sounded even closer. I yelped in fright as something bashed against the trapdoor and then roared.

My eyes snapped open and I was staring at an old yellowish photo of a man in a white pointy helmet standing with his foot on a tiger. He had a big gun in one hand, and was smoking a pipe with the other. I knew whom it was from the dangly moustache: Wesley J. Harding.

There was more pounding on the trapdoor. It bounced in the opening, and the bolt rattled. I knew I was still safe, though. The trapdoor opened outwards, so no amount of hammering was going to help. If it was Dad, he'd know all he had to do was unbolt it and lower the cover. But maybe it *was* him, only he might be like Mum had been. She'd looked the same as normal, except for the dribble and the milky eyes. Maybe them things weren't too clever. Maybe they were too thick to work a bolt. Even so, I knew I couldn't take chances. I had to think, and think quick. I needed a weapon.

Next to the picture of Wesley J. Harding there was a wad of cloth all tied up with string. I lifted it out, surprised at how heavy it was. I nearly dropped it when the banging got louder and the wood of the trapdoor started to split. I fumbled at the string, pulling it over the edges of the bundle because I couldn't untie the knots. As I began to unwrap the material, it suddenly went quiet below. I heard the bolt being turned; heard it snap back. Acid came up my throat, almost made me sick. I dropped the bundle and something heavy thudded against the boards.

A gun.

It was pistol-like thing with one of those chambers like I had on my Nerf gun. It looked really old. Really, really old. There was a strange thrill as I curled my fingers around the handle and lifted it with both hands. *How do you open it?* I thought, trying to remember what they did in those cowboy films Dad made me watch. I fiddled with the chamber but couldn't budge it. Would it still work? Did it have any bullets? Would I be thrown back through the wall if it went off, 'cause I was only a kid, and kids don't fire guns?

Light beamed up from below as the trapdoor fell open. I scrambled back on my bum, holding Wesley J. Harding's gun so tight my knuckles went white. I inched back further, never taking my eyes off the entrance, my heart pounding so loud I couldn't hear anything else. A hand reached over the edge, then another. It was Dad, I knew it. I could see his wedding ring glinting in the dirty light. When his head popped up, I nearly dropped the gun and went to him. My whole body ached to be held. Dad must've killed that thing down there; must've come to rescue me. But then his head turned toward me and I saw his eyes. They were just like Mum's— all white and empty. He roared and sprayed spit and slobber everywhere. He started to drag his body through the opening, hissing and growling. My arms were shaking from holding the gun; my head was bursting with tears and fear and sadness and loneliness and-and-and—

Click.

Nothing happened.

I pulled the trigger again. Just another click. Nothing. There were no bullets. There was no magic. *I hate you, Wesley J. Harding. I hate you!*

I screamed and threw the gun with all my strength. It smacked into Dad's head and splatted it like a melon. He dropped back through the opening and there was a thud, a crack, and a slosh. I had to see. I had to see what had happened. So I crawled on hands and knees to the opening and peered over the edge. Dad was lying in a sprawled heap on top of a smashed up chair. There was blood all around his head, and his legs were twisted at a horrible angle. Then I was sick, really sick, when I saw the bone poking through his jeans, the chair leg sticking out of his chest, drip, drip, dripping blood. A stream of my yucky brown puke rained down on him and he growled. His head twisted to glare at me with dead eyes, and his fingers scratched at the carpet. He reached a hand up and clawed the air, roaring at me and gnashing his teeth.

I drew back from the edge and stood. I knew he couldn't get up, not with his legs all broken like that, but I didn't want to chance it. I took hold of the canvas wardrobe at the top and pulled. It was real heavy, so I tried again, using more of my bodyweight. It rocked and then tipped right over the opening. Clothes fell out and flopped down below. Dad growled some more, but he was muffled now, buried under Mum's cast-offs. The wardrobe sagged, but covered the opening good enough.

I noticed Wesley J. Harding's gun up against the wall where it had bounced off of Dad's head. I narrowed my eyes at it and screwed my nose up. But then I sighed and gave it a nod of respect. It might not have worked, but it had saved me anyway. Maybe Wesley J. Harding was on my side after all.

I decided if I was gonna get out of this alive, I needed to do some rummaging. Maybe there'd be some rope so I could do that rope-trick thing Wesley J. used to do. Dad said the rope would go stiff and Wesley J. would climb right up into the clouds. I started going through some old suitcases that were stacked along the sides, but they were mostly filled with more of Mum's old clothes. She had so many clothes, my Mum, but most of them didn't fit anymore. She did lots of silly things, Dad said, like going to Weight Watchers and then ordering Chinese; or telling Dad to hide the scales so she couldn't weigh herself every day, and then messing up the whole house trying to find them. She'd moan about having all this junk food in the cupboards because she couldn't stop herself from eating it, even though she was the one who bought it in the first place.

Tears were pouring from my eyes and snot ran over my lips and onto my chin. I missed her, my big silly Mummy. I really missed her. And Daddy, my best friend in the whole world. I needed him now like never before. If he were here, everything would be all right. We could find a way to beat these zombies. I know we could.

"Shut up," I said to myself. "Ain't got time to whine. No one's gonna save you, so stop acting like a baby."

That reminded me of something Dad used to say to me if I was blubbing for no good reason. "Stop crying, or I'll give you something to cry about," he'd say. It always sounded mean at the time, but I'd have given anything to hear him say it now.

There was a groan from down below, and this time it was answered by growling from outside. I got closer to the low part of the ceiling and tried to listen. It was still raining, but it had slowed to a steady pitter patter. The thunder had rolled off into the distance; there were just occasional rumbles, and they were getting further apart. I couldn't hear the policemen shouting anymore; couldn't hear their gunshots either. Just the horrid wails of the zombies. No one was even screaming now.

I pulled myself together and moved on past Mum's clothes. I brought down a cardboard box that had been sealed up with tape. As I did, something squeaked, and I heard the trip trap of tiny feet. *Ain't got time to worry about mice*, I thought as I ripped the tape from the box and looked inside. It was crammed full of toys. Old toys I'd never seen before. Perhaps they were Dad's childhood things that he'd kept in case I wanted them. Maybe he was secretly collecting stuff to give me for Christmas. He'd done that last year, when I got all these really cool Cylons, and a phaser from the original *Star Trek*.

I pulled out an action figure. He had on a red suit and trainers, and he had a see-through eye. I squinted through it and saw things a little bigger. One of his arms had rubber skin over it. It was a bit split and hard in places, but I managed to roll it up. There were colourful pretend electronics underneath, like he had a robot arm or something. Dad had a real robot arm. He got it when his old arm was bit off by a great white shark, he said. Bionic, it was. Looked just the same as a normal one, only it was super strong. If Watson had bit that one, Dad might still be OK. He could've used it to clobber down the zombies, no matter how many came at us. With that arm, he'd have picked them up and thrown them so high in the air they'd have hit the moon.

I put the figure on the floor and lifted another box. This one rattled a lot, and when I opened it I saw it was full of Lego bricks. I was about to put it to one side when I remembered building this enormous castle in the living room when I was five or six. Dad helped me, and it took days, it was so big. Mum kept complaining she couldn't do the Hoovering while it was there, but I think she must've liked it because she let us keep it for a week or so.

I took out a block and set it on the floor. I hummed a tune to drown out the groaning from the street, and began to stack brick upon brick. It was odd, 'cause I didn't really know what I was making. I just kept piling the bricks up, one on top of another, and as I worked I heard words in between my ears, getting louder and louder—songs Dad used to play on the stereo.

Guess who just got back today. It was his voice, all scratchy and kind of silly.

Them wild eyed boys that had been away.

Mum's voice cut across the singing. It was that screechy way she yelled "Dinner's ready." I half stood, started to call back, but there was a lump in my throat that slowly sunk all the way down to my belly.

Haven't changed, haven't much to say, but man I still think them cats are crazy.

My hands moved faster and faster, stacking the bricks higher and higher as the song built up to the chorus. That was the bit I used to sing along to, and me and Dad both would dance around playing air guitars.

The boys are back in town.
The boys are back in town.
The boys are back in town.

We were always the boys who were back in town. We'd do this thing with our Nerf guns where we'd jump out of the car and lock and load. I could see it in my head, me and Dad fighting off hundreds and hundreds of monsters—you know, Magog or Cybermen; Daleks or the creepy Borg.

A crash from downstairs startled me out of my daydream.

Glass.

Breaking glass.

Then I heard angry growls and the sound of wood snapping and splintering. I knew if I could just keep focused I wouldn't get scared. I watched my fingers picking up blocks of Lego and placing them on whatever it was I was building like they had a mind of their own. I worked quickly, brick upon brick, Dad's silly songs running 'round my head and making me laugh and cry, and miss him and Mum so much it felt like my organs were all dropping out of my body. I cried and cried, but they were someone else's tears, and the people I saw—Nanny and Granddad, Aunty Paula and Uncle Del, even my best friend Joe Molloy, they all looked like they'd been cut out of a comic.

Kings of speed, we're gonna make you kings of speed, Dad sang. Smash, crash, bash went the creatures downstairs.

The ace of spades, the ace of spades. Moan, groan, moan, groan.

The thing that used to be Dad roared, and the things downstairs roared back. I cried out loud then. I still wanted to go to him, even though I knew he was gone. I didn't want to be on my own. I didn't want them to get me.

Something squealed and I looked up. Two beady white eyes were watching me from the shadows. I threw a Lego brick at them and they vanished for a second, only to reappear a few feet away. I picked up another brick and placed it on whatever it was I was building. Somehow I knew it was finished. I pushed back and stood so I could see it better. It was a rectangle, like a doorframe for a dwarf. It stood on a chunky base of stepped bricks and had a shiny piece like a lamp on top. I was about to see if I could walk through it when more beady eyes lit up beyond the doorway.

I stepped away and looked around for something I could use to frighten them off. The yellow plastic of one of my old Nerf guns caught my eye. I pushed past some boxes and grabbed it. It was the one with the revolving chamber and a full load of foam darts. I cocked it, spun round, and fired at the first pair of white eyes. There was a squeak and they disappeared. More and more eyes were appearing all over the attic. Some of them scurried out into the light and I kept turning to make sure they didn't sneak up on me.

Rats.

Dozens of them, all filthy and frothing at the mouth. They were squealing at me, staring me down with milky eyes just like Watson's. Just like Mum's. Just like Dad's.

There were heavy footsteps on the stairs and more moaning and groaning. I fired off another Nerf dart and one of the rats scarpered. The others kept closing in, hissing and baring their yellow teeth. Something roared below on the landing and then light spilled up through the trapdoor opening as the canvas wardrobe was pulled down. Fingers grabbed the edge of the opening, but they slipped away. There was a thud as the thing must've hit the ground, but straight away more fingers took hold of the edge. I'd taken my eyes off the rats, and when I looked back they'd got even closer. I shot one right on the nose, but I could see it was no good. More and more were crawling over the attic junk and coming at me from all sides. I fired again and then threw the gun at a pack of them.

A head appeared through the trapdoor opening and the most evil face I'd ever seen snarled at me. Long ropes of drool dangled from its chin as it thrashed about crazily and started to drag itself into the attic. More hands appeared behind it, and below I could hear so much moaning that I knew the house must be full of zombies.

I kicked a rat that had got too close and turned, looking for somewhere to run. They were everywhere, spitting and hissing, squeaking and scratching. The first zombie was finding its feet, while the next was halfway into the attic. I screamed, whirling around desperately and knowing one of the rats was gonna bite me any second. There was no more being grown up, no more being brave. I wanted Mummy. I wanted Daddy, and there was no one. Maybe there was no one anywhere. I tottered and nearly fell, and when I steadied myself I saw a strange violet glow. It was coming from the Lego doorway. I stared at it, openmouthed, even as cold fingers touched the back of my neck. The rats swarmed toward me in waves, and the fingers started to dig into my skin. I screamed again and broke away, tripping on a big rat and falling headlong through the doorway. I hit my head hard and it all went black.

* * *

There was a buzzing in my ears, like someone had stuck me in a wasps' nest. Everything itched and prickled and ached and burned. I was cold, then hot, then cold again. Mum was standing in the doorway, holding out a bag of shopping for me to take.

"Chain gang time," Dad said, leaning over my shoulder to kiss Mum on the lips. The second they touched, it all went fuzzy. My head spun like I was in a washing machine and I ended up face down in bed. *Bad dream*, I thought and tried to pull the covers up, only there weren't any covers.

I let out a whimper and tried to move. There was something gritty in my mouth. I spat and raised my head to see what it was.

Dirt.

I was lying face down in dirt. There were trees all around me; tall scraggly trees with no leaves. Heavy clouds hung in the sky and big birds flitted in and out of the treetops. I started at the sound of crunching footsteps getting closer and closer.

"Steady now, old chap," a man's voice said. It was so gruff it sounded like he needed a good cough to clear his throat.

I twisted my head to look up at him. At first he was just a blurry blob of white, but as I blinked, a pointy helmet came into focus. He bent down, resting his weight on a rifle. I rolled onto my back and sat up. I smelled something whiskeyish on his breath, and there were crumbs of food on his dangly moustache. His eyes were sparkly blue with magic, and his cheeks were red and blotchy.

"Good show, old man," he said. "Good show."

"I …. but … I … omigosh! Wesley J. Harding! But this can't be … This isn't real."

Wesley J. Harding's brows knitted together and his eyes lost their shine for a moment.

"You could say that, I suppose. Yes, you could say that." He twiddled his moustache and the sparkle returned to his eyes. "Come on, laddie. Can't dally. Tiger-men on the tail, what, and you don't want them to catch you in the open, mark my word."

He took hold of my elbow and led me off through the trees toward the red disk of the setting sun. I had a zillion questions, but he started to run and it took all my breath just to keep up.

"Tell me, laddie," he called over his shoulder. "Have you ever tried a bed of nails? Look like you could use a good sleep, what."

"Sleep?" I said. "I can't sleep."

He stopped and took me by the shoulders, nodding and frowning.

"I know, laddie. Forgive an old codger. Course you can't sleep after what you've been through."

I pulled back from him, all tensed up and ready for a fight.

"No, it's not that. I'm hungry, is what. Really, really hungry. Starving."

"Ah," Wesley J. said, slapping the barrel of his rifle. "And I think I know just what you need."

I was already licking my lips, somehow knowing what he was gonna say. It felt like someone had lit a fire cracker in my tummy and filled my veins with pepper. My mouth was all squelchy and full of spit that dribbled down my chin. There was a hole in my stomach the size of the Grand Canyon and nothing was gonna make it go away.

"Come on, laddie." Wesley J. turned around, sniffing the air and raising his rifle to his eye. "Let's go hunt ourselves some tiger-men."

D.P. Prior *is an author and editor working in the South of England. He has a background in the performing arts as an actor, director, and playwright. He is a founder member of the legendary rock band Sergeant Sunshine and has written and recorded countless songs. He has extensive experience as a mental health professional and has studied theatre, film, classics, history and theology at bachelors and masters levels.*

He runs his own editing service with his wife, Paula:
www.homunculuseditingservices.blogspot.com

He is also the author of the Shader *series, which includes* Cadman's Gambit *and* Best Laid Plans. *He has also written* The Chronicles of the Nameless Dwarf—*including* The Ant-Man of Malfen *and* The Axe of the Dwarf Lords. *Also in his library is* Thanatos Rising *from* The Memoirs of Harry Chesterton.

For all things Shader please visit: www.deaconshader.blogspot.com

For The Nameless Dwarf, please visit: www.namelessdwarf.blogspot.com

Facebook page: www.facebook.com/derek.prior1

NIGHT NIGHT

by Daniel Pyle

Early Saturday morning, before the sun rose, before the birds woke and started their new-day chirping, Henry Clement pulled a steak knife from his pocket, watched the dim light from the beside lamp reflect off the blade, and then leaned over his sleeping brother and stabbed him six times in the throat.

It was a messy, amateurish job, but he had expected that. He'd never killed anyone before.

The first thrust barely penetrated the flesh on the side of Jerry's neck. Jerry started to scream, to thrash. Henry put more muscle into it, and the second two stabs went deeper, turned the screams into soft gurgles. Those three wounds probably would have been enough, but Henry punched the knife in three more times anyway. Just to be sure.

Blood spurted from Jerry's neck, pooled on the pillow and mattress around his head. He slapped a hand against the punctures and looked at Henry with wide, disbelieving eyes, like he must have been dreaming this. His hand slipped through the blood and fell to his side. He lay there for what seemed like a very long time, flopping, unable to breathe, a man-fish. And then he let out a final, wet cough, spraying more blood across his already-drenched chest, and stopped breathing. Deflated. Dead.

Splattered blood dripped down Henry's face and across his nostrils and lips. A particularly heavy spurt had hit him across his chest and left a crimson mark from his shoulder to his hip. Like a sash.

Henry dropped the knife on the mattress.

"I'm sorry," he said and kissed Jerry on the forehead. His lips left a bloody print between his brother's eyebrows. Tears streamed down Henry's face, sluicing through the blood and dripping onto Jerry's neck and shoulders.

Henry wiped his eyes and stared past the body, through the bedroom window. Still dark, of course. Nowhere close to daylight. Mandy would be by to see them sometime today. She might arrive

43

as early as ten o'clock, after she'd fed her children breakfast and sent them off with her husband on some kind of adventure, or she might wait until after lunch, until the whole lot of them returned home from the zoo or the park or a matinee. Whether she continued to come because she wanted to or because she felt it was her sisterly duty, Henry didn't know, but she never missed a weekend.

Still, whether it was before lunch or after, it didn't really matter. Henry had never worn a watch, and there was no clock in the bedroom, but he guessed it couldn't have been any later than four in the morning. That left him plenty of time to do what needed doing.

He grabbed Jerry's arm and pulled-jerked-rolled him off the bed. They fell to the floor together. Jerry's face smacked the hardwood with a juicy thud, and Henry fell on top of him, panting. He wasn't exactly a weakling, but he hadn't realized how hard it would be to move Jerry's corpse.

Dead weight.

He ain't heavy. He's your brother.

He considered dragging Jerry into the bathroom, pulling him into the shower and washing off the blood. Except what would be the point? The blood was gruesome, sure, but washing away the gore would reveal the stab wounds, and he doubted those would be any less horrific.

No. No shower. Let the doctors or the undertaker or whoever was in charge of such things worry about the cleanup.

He got up, lifting Jerry to a standing position, and backed across the room, looking over Jerry's shoulder at the bloodied bed sheets. So much blood. He'd expected a lot, had visualized it repeatedly, but he guessed he hadn't been prepared for the reality. He stopped once, halfway across the bedroom, steadied Jerry, and vomited on the floor between Jerry's feet.

"Sorry, man," he said. As if Jerry could hear. As if the puking had been Henry's worst offense of the day.

He spat out the last bit of bile and dragged Jerry the rest of the way across the room, looking everywhere but at the bed.

In the hall, their parents stared down at them from wall-hung photos—old portraits with the couple looking young and bright eyed and ready to face the world, newer pictures in which they appeared tired, wrinkled around the eyes, disappointed. Henry thought they would have understood why he did what he'd done, if not approved.

NIGHT NIGHT

He dragged Jerry past the bathroom, leaving red footprints on the rug and all kinds of bloody smears on the walls, stumbling, grunting, sweating.

Getting down the stairs was going to be the hard part. Henry pictured himself stumbling on the first step, crashing end over end to the landing below, paralyzed, Jerry's corpse on top of him, pressing down on his lungs, suffocating him.

He took a deep breath, bit his bottom lip, and dragged Jerry down the first step. For a second, he thought it was going to happen exactly as he'd imagined. His foot slid to the edge of the step, and gravity tugged at him. He grabbed the railing, let Jerry's body slump against him, and managed to keep his balance. Barely. He stood there for at least a minute, fingers wrapped around the handrail, panting, afraid that even the smallest movement would send the two of them over the tipping point and into a bone-crushing tumble. Jerry's head flopped to the side, and suddenly Henry was looking into a dead, glazed eye.

Henry shivered and closed his own eyes. His arm trembled, and he knew he couldn't hold on to the railing forever. Adrenaline and determination had gotten him this far, but he could feel exhaustion creeping in. A physical and mental drain. Keeping his eyes closed, he backed down one more step. His heart thumped irregularly, and for a second he thought he must be feeling both their hearts, his and Jerry's. Except that was ridiculous. He was psyching himself out. He needed to stop thinking and start moving.

He backed down another step, and Jerry's head flopped again. This time, his lips pressed against Henry's neck. Like a kiss. Once upon a time, a much younger Jerry had kissed Henry goodnight every evening before bed. Henry remembered the feel of Jerry's mouth on his cheek, remembered him saying *Night night, Bubby. See you in the morning.* Those were the words he'd fallen asleep to for many years. After their parents had gone to bed. After the lights were off. *Night night, Bubby. See you in the morning.*

Now Jerry's lips felt lifeless, rubbery, like the lips on a Halloween mask after a long, cold night of trick-or-treating.

Henry wanted to shift his brother, to get the lips off his neck, but he didn't dare try it. He'd just have to deal with it until he made it to flat ground. He eased Jerry down another step, groaned, paused, and then repeated the process.

By the time he reached the first floor, Henry's chest was damp with sweat and he was shaking uncontrollably. He thought he'd be able to drag Jerry through the living room and kitchen and out onto the back porch, but after that, he expected his body to give up on him. And that was fine. The back porch was as far as he needed to get.

Off the stairs and no longer in any danger of falling any farther than the distance from his head to the floor, Henry managed to ease Jerry's lips off his neck. He dragged his brother away from the staircase, through the narrow entryway at the front of the house, and past the living-room sofa. He paused for a second at an end table and grabbed an old photo album from the drawer. He stuffed this in the waistband of his pants and moved on.

In the kitchen, he glanced toward the block of knives, now one short. He'd tucked the blade into his pocket the night before when they were doing dishes, snuck it when Jerry turned away to put a stack of dry plates in the cupboard. For a second, Henry thought Jerry had seen what he was doing—maybe caught his reflection in the toaster oven's little glass door—but if he had seen, Jerry hadn't said anything, and saying nothing had never exactly been his style.

Henry pulled his brother's body around the small kitchen table, through the back door, and onto the porch.

* * *

"What would you do?" Jerry said. They sat on the couch on the back porch, reading. Jerry sat on the right—always on the right—with his foot up on the coffee table between a stack of old magazines and a tower of empty soda cans. He held his Kindle between two fingers and stared intently at the screen.

"That's not a complete sentence."

Now Jerry looked up. "Come on. Seriously. What would you do?"

"What would I do if what?" Henry put down his own Kindle and frowned.

"If..." He bit his lip. "You know...if I died."

Henry rolled his eyes. "Let's not start that again."

"Why not?" Jerry said. "It's a valid question."

"It's a stupid *question. You're not gonna die. Okay? Not anytime soon anyway."*

"You heard what the doct—"

"Phhhhh." Henry rolled his eyes. "The doctor? What's he know? He couldn't find his dick with both hands and a microscope."

46

Jerry smiled but didn't laugh. "It's not a stupid question. I just want to know what you'd do."

"I'd cry my eyes out, okay," Henry said. "Is that what you wanna hear?"

"It's a start."

Henry punched him on the shoulder. "You know what I'd really do?"

"What?"

"I'd come out here and read alone," said Henry, "and enjoy the fucking peace and quiet."

* * *

On the back porch, under the glow of the single, low-wattage bulb, Henry lowered Jerry's body to the wicker sofa and dropped down beside him, wheezing. The veins in his neck and head throbbed. He felt hot, dizzy.

He pulled the photo album out of his waistband and laid it across his leg, but before he opened it, he took a second to catch his breath and let his heart slow.

Exercise much? Jerry said.

Henry's eyes flew open, and he turned to his brother. Jerry stared back at him with his dead, milky eyes.

I didn't just hear that, Henry thought. *Of course not. That was just my imagination. Or my guilt. Or both.*

He watched Jerry for what felt like several minutes, knowing he wouldn't move, wouldn't speak, but half expecting him to anyway. In the dark yard beyond the porch, crickets chirped. Somewhere in the distance, a vehicle that must have been an eighteen-wheeler or a large truck sped by.

Henry cupped his hand around the side of Jerry's face and gave it a gentle shake.

"Jer?"

Jerry said nothing.

"Brother?"

Still nothing.

Henry shook his head. He'd caught his breath, but his heart hadn't stopped pounding. Maybe it never would.

He opened to the first page of the photo album, to a picture that showed young Henry and Jerry in a small, backyard pool. Mandy stood just outside the pool, maybe running around the perimeter, maybe getting ready to jump in and splash her little

47

brothers. All three of them had huge smiles plastered across their faces, but Jerry's was widest of all.

I always loved playing in that pool, Jerry said.

Henry ignored this and flipped to the next page.

* * *

Henry took out one of Jerry's knights with his last pawn, simultaneously shielding his bishop from Jerry's queen.

"Suck on that," Henry said.

Jerry groaned.

While he waited for Jerry to make his move, Henry stared into the back yard. A couple of birds landed on the rusted T-pole that was the last of the pair that had once held the old clothesline. Henry tried to imagine a world in which people had the time or inclination to haul whole loads of wash into the back yard for air-drying and couldn't quite do it.

"If it comes down to it," Jerry said, "I don't want to suffer."

"Huh?"

Jerry repeated himself.

"Uh...duh," Henry said. "You think there are people out there who do want to suffer?" He didn't look away from the birds, didn't quite understand what Jerry had said until his brain had a second to run through it again.

"Probably," Jerry said. "But I'm not one of them."

Now Henry looked at his brother. "Are you seriously talking about this again? I thought I—"

"I have to talk about it. No matter how much you want to pretend it isn't happening, I need to face reality. We need to."

Henry said nothing.

"If it comes down to it," Jerry repeated, "I don't want to suffer. But I don't think I have the guts to...well, you know."

"Yeah," Henry said. "I know. Try not to worry about it, okay? Now shut up and make your damn move."

* * *

Henry flipped to a picture from some birthday party or other. In it, both he and Jerry had cake smeared across their faces. Mandy wasn't in this one, although she had undoubtedly been nearby. It might even have been her party. Henry couldn't remember for sure.

NIGHT NIGHT

It was *her party,* Jerry said. *We gave her a doll, remember? That stupid doll she carried around from then on? She probably still has that thing on a shelf in her bedroom.*

And suddenly—thanks to Jerry, or the Jerry in his imagination—Henry *did* remember.

Henry plopped his foot onto the coffee table and kicked over a pile of papers. One of those sheets held Jerry's test results. They had looked over the results together when they got home from the doctor's office, pretending to understand what they meant.

But they hadn't really needed to understand the science; the doctor had laid it out in plain old English:

Jerry is going to die, he'd said, leaning forward in his leather chair and staring at them through his thick, Santa Claus glasses. *Not today, and not tomorrow, and probably not in the next few months, but within the year for sure. And we need to start planning what we're going to do.*

There'd been no need to plan, of course. Not really. Jerry had already made his feelings perfectly clear.

I don't want to suffer, he'd said. *But I don't think I have the guts to kill myself if that's what it comes to.*

Jerry hadn't said that last part, but he hadn't needed to say it outright. Brothers—really close brothers—have more than one kind of communication.

The doctor hadn't said what he thought might happen to Henry, hadn't even been willing to give them his best guess.

Henry knew now, however. He could feel himself weakening, could sense the world closing in around him like a big, warm blanket.

He turned to the last page of the photo album.

The picture showed him and Jerry on stage at one of the many carnivals they'd toured over the years. The banner above them said, in big white letters, MEET JERRY AND HENRY, THE AMAZING SIAMESE TWINS!

Political incorrectness aside, Henry thought it was a nice picture. It showed the two of them in mid-bow, smiling out at the audience with their twin grins.

He closed the album and laid his head on their conjoined shoulder. He hoped Mandy would be okay with this, that she'd get over it in time.

She will, Jerry said. *She's tough.*

Henry smiled. In the end, he hadn't gotten the peace and quiet he'd often longed for—not so much as a single minute of alone time in his entire life—but that was okay. He thought maybe isolation was overrated.

In the trees beyond the porch, a single bird woke and sang. It was still too early for so much as a hint of sunlight on the eastern horizon, but it would come soon enough.

Henry leaned his head into Jerry's neck and ignored the stench of blood.

Night night, Bubby.

Henry kissed his brother's cheek. "Night night," he said and closed his eyes for the last time.

Daniel Pyle *is the author of* Dismember, Down the Drain, Freeze, *the upcoming* Man vs. Himself, *and many short stories. He is also the editor of* Unnatural Disasters *and is an Active member of the Horror Writers Association. After studying creative writing at Amherst College, he moved back to his hometown of Springfield, Missouri, where he now lives with his wife and two daughters. You can visit him online at www.danielpyle.com.*

NIGHT NIGHT

DEAD THINGS

by Michael Crane

When he heard the doorbell, Dwight rubbed his face with his hands. A loud, disheartened sigh left his lips. He knew one of his least favorite people in the world would be at the door. He didn't hate her, of course. He knew the woman had issues that were beyond her control, but after a few months of this it was becoming a tired trend.

After taking a breath, he finally went to the door and answered it. "Everything okay, Mrs. Hendrickson?"

The old woman wore a horrid pink robe decorated with blackbirds. She shook her wrinkly head while her mouth quivered. "Zombies, Mr. Jacobs! Zombies."

He did his best to hold in a groan. For weeks Mrs. Hendrickson had been coming over, claiming zombies had invaded their cozy little town and was convinced it would only be a matter of time before they tracked her down. She even went into graphic detail about what zombies did to people, even though Dwight was quite aware of how they behaved due to many of the horror flicks he'd watched over the years. Of course, he didn't believe her. She was probably off her meds again.

"Zombies?" Dwight asked. "Have you been watching scary movies again?"

Mrs. Hendrickson's mouth hung agape and an offended gasp escaped her throat. She wagged her finger at him. "Don't you go making fun of me, sonny boy. I'm trying to tell you something important here. Zombies are invading our neighborhood!"

He took a quick peek outside and threw his hands up. "I don't see anything, Mrs. Hendrickson. Maybe you were dreaming?"

"Fine," she said, putting her hands on her hips. "Don't believe me. Think I'm a wacko. I'm sure that's what everyone thinks of me anyway."

"Nobody thinks you're a wacko," Dwight said, although he damn well knew that was a lie. The whole neighborhood knew of Mrs. Hendrickson's antics, though they never complained or confronted her about it. Everybody felt sorry for her after she lost her husband in a car accident two years ago. That was when she really started to go off the deep end. She would keep herself locked up in her house and do nothing but watch TV all day long. No wonder she came up with such outrageous stories.

Dwight began to rub his arms even though he wasn't cold. "It's getting late. If you see any zombies lurking about, you can come back and let me know."

She waved him off, angrily shaking her head. "Whatever. I know you're mocking me, but I'm gonna show you once and for all that there are zombies and I'm not off my rocker!" He watched her storm away while she continued to shake her head and mumble to herself. Dwight just stared in silence. He hoped she wouldn't come back again, but he wasn't that lucky of a guy. She *always* came back. After taking one last look outside, he closed the door.

"Was that Mrs. Hendrickson again?"

Dwight turned and saw his seven-year-old son, Jimmy, standing on the stairs. He wore his blue pajamas, his brown hair a feathery mess on the left side of his head.

"You should be in bed."

"Is it true? Did she really see zombies?" Jimmy asked.

"No, she didn't see any zombies." Dwight ran his hand through his son's hair and the two of them began to walk up the stairs. "You know she has problems."

"What kind of problems?"

"She's not really right in the head, you know? I mean, she lost her husband and she's a bit on the old side." He cringed at his own words, knowing that he wasn't the best when it came to explaining things to his son or giving fatherly speeches.

"Old people have problems?" Jimmy asked while Dwight tucked him in.

"Some of them do. When something really bad happened, or when they get old, they start to act like a child. I think it's a little bit of both when it comes to Mrs. Hendrickson."

One of Jimmy's eyes became big. "She's turning into a kid?"

Dwight chuckled and shook his head. "Not like that. In her head, she's thinking more and more like a kid."

"And that's bad?"

"When you're a grownup like her it is. There's nothing to be afraid of. She won't hurt you or anything. It's just that she's a little out of it and she makes up stories. It's her mind playing tricks on her. When she tells these stories, she thinks they're true, but they really aren't."

"So there's no zombies?"

"Only in movies." When he noticed that Jimmy's eyes shrunk and a worried frown began to spread across his face, he asked, "What's the matter? I'm sorry if she scared you, but it's really nothing—"

"It's not that."

"What is it, then?"

Jimmy's tiny nose crinkled a bit. "Mommy looked like a zombie sometimes."

A chill ran through Dwight. His shoulders twitched at the thought of Sammie. The frail and sickly image of her burned into his mind, and no matter how much he wanted to he couldn't shake it away. He could never get her out of his head, but the days that passed without a mention of her were considered good days. There was no denying that his son was right about such a comparison. By the end of their marriage she had transformed into a gaunt shell of what she used to be, her skin pale as bones, those horrible, rotting teeth. She wasn't the same woman he had fallen in love with, that was for sure.

"Enough zombie talk," Dwight said. He gave Jimmy a soft kiss on his forehead and pinched his right cheek while saying goodnight. He left the bedroom, leaving the door open a crack. He stood outside of Jimmy's room for several minutes, motionless.

* * *

Sammie had become a meth addict. While Dwight never figured out what triggered it, he had always suspected that it was because she wasn't ready to be a mother. It was like a part of her life was over and she did everything she could to hold onto that part, never growing up or accepting any responsibility. Sure, she enjoyed being a mother at first, but her depression started when Jimmy was a year old. She would slump in a chair with her hands over her face, crying, ignoring her son's pleas. Dwight had suggested they take a vacation, saying how his father always looked forward to watching over Jimmy while they were away. The offer never seemed to appeal to her. That's when he thought maybe *he* was the problem.

She started going out regularly with friends not too long after that. As soon as Dwight would step into the house, before even saying, "I'm home," she would rush out the door, all dressed up with gallons of makeup on her face. She wouldn't come home until late in the morning the next day. Dwight was pretty sure she'd cheated on him, but he never confronted her. In the end he just wanted to be there for Jimmy, but it tore him apart having the youngster ask him every night where his mommy was.

"She went out," he'd tell him.

That's when Jimmy would frown and say, "Mommy goes out a lot."

He didn't know what else to say. At first he figured Sammie was burnt out on motherhood and needed to escape for a while. He told himself that it was a phase and she'd snap out of it. If he pressed her on the issue or got mad, it'd only make things worse. He figured that if he just let her do as she pleased, she'd get bored and drop the act.

Dwight could've never imagined that it would get as bad as it did. When she started rapidly losing weight, that's when he knew that something was up. She wasn't the same person anymore, constantly indifferent to everything. Whenever Dwight asked her a question, she'd mumble an unintelligible reply. She stayed away from the house more and more, even when he was at work. It got to a point where Dwight would have to call his father and ask him to watch Jimmy during the day.

"Son, you know your wife's got a serious problem," his father said at one point.

Dwight had told him everything was under control. His father agreed to look after Jimmy while he was at work. Dwight wasn't exactly pleased that it had to happen that way, but he didn't know what else could be done.

When Dwight came home from work one night, his father sat him down at the table so they could have a talk. Dwight knew this wouldn't be a pleasant conversation, but he had nowhere else he could go, and he knew that his father wouldn't leave until he said what he needed to say.

"You've got to face that fact that your wife has a problem, Dwight. You can't keep on denying it."

"Who's denying it? I know things aren't good."

"But you're not doing anything about it."

56

Dwight threw his hands in the air. "Dad, what the hell am I supposed to do? Huh? Sammie is an adult, and I can't ground her for acting out."

"This goes beyond acting out, Son."

"She'll snap out of it."

"She's a mother, for chrissakes!"

"I know what she is."

"Clearly you don't. Last time I saw her, she looked like a walking corpse. And her teeth!"

"Dad..."

"You know she has a drug problem. There's not much else that can cause a body to change like that."

Dwight rubbed his face into his hands. His eyes began to water, but he did his damndest to fight back the tears. Yes, he knew what was going on with Sammie. It didn't take a rocket scientist to figure it out. Maybe he didn't want to face it because he felt responsible. He should've stopped it long before it got so out of hand, but he really believed that Sammie would get better on her own. Anything was better than Sammie leaving them.

"Dad," he started, "when you and Mom had problems, you tried to talk it out with her. And you two split."

"We had problems, but nothing like what you're dealing with. And even though we split, we never stopped being your parents, now did we? You can't sit there and be passive just because you're afraid Sammie is going to walk out on you."

"I don't want to lose her."

"She's not Sammie, Dwight. She's...something else. The woman you loved is gone, but there's a way to get her back. She's gotta get clean. Seek treatment. Threaten to cut her off from you and Jimmy."

"And if she walks?"

His father shrugged. "Then that's what it's gotta be."

He knew his father was right—he always was—but that didn't make the issue any easier on him. He couldn't envision a life without Sammie, even if she was different. Still, he knew things had to change for the better soon. Jimmy had started asking him questions about her appearance. He might've been little, but he was no dummy. Dwight couldn't bring himself to tell his son the truth. Something had to be done.

On an evening when Sammie walked into the house well past midnight, Dwight was waiting for her in the living room. He told her they needed to talk. Her eyes were half-closed and her blond hair looked like dried hay.

"What about?" she asked, emotionless.

"You've got a problem."

She brought her boney finger to her nose and gave a loud snort. "Yeah? Took you long enough to notice."

"I've known for a while. I just thought you were going through some weird phase, that you'd snap out of it."

"There's nothing to snap out of."

"I mean, I know you're unhappy," he continued. "I thought if I gave you some space things would somehow go back to normal. I just didn't think you'd..." He couldn't finish the sentence. His guilt pounded him in his gut. He closed his eyes and counted to three, willing himself to be strong.

"You need help," Dwight finally said after a moment of uncomfortable silence. "Seriously, I want you to check into rehab."

Sammie stared at him with dead eyes. She sniffled loudly and rubbed her jaw. "Yeah? What if I don't want to go?"

"If you won't go, then you can't be around Jimmy and me anymore."

"And you're serious?"

Dwight nodded.

She continued to stare at him, no emotion to be found on her pale face. She shrugged her bone-thin shoulders. "I want a divorce," was all she said to him before she left the house. She never looked back or said goodbye.

*　*　*

Dwight sat in his chair, drinking a beer. The memory of Sammie left a bitter taste in his mouth. There were times he wondered what she was up to, but he knew she was probably dead somewhere. It wasn't a pleasant thought, and it hurt, but it was probably the truth. He didn't wish it and he certainly didn't hate her, but he was angry that she had abandoned them. He was also angry with himself for not doing anything sooner.

During the divorce, Sammie didn't want money. She didn't even want to fight for custody or visitation rights. She simply wanted *out*.

Jimmy took it hard at first, but he was a bright kid. He knew that Mommy wasn't herself and needed help. For a while he would ask Dwight if he thought she would get better and come back. He didn't lie and tell him she would, nor did he tell him the truth and say she wouldn't. He simply said he didn't know.

Those questions came with less and less frequency each passing day.

Even though she was gone, Sammie was never that far from his thoughts. No matter how hard he tried to forget her, there she was. Whenever he thought of her, he'd put the blame on himself. He knew he should've tried harder. He should've confronted her at the first sign of a problem, but that's how life goes. Even when the warning signs are there, sometimes people are still afraid to fess up.

A loud banging at the front door startled him. Dwight jumped up from his chair, nearly dropping his beer. "Jesus!" he moaned. It was a violent chain of thuds, and in between each of them he heard a whiney voice call out his name.

"Oh God," he said. "Not this again."

He wiped the beer from his lips and set the can down. At the door he found an excited Mrs. Hendrickson.

"Really? I have no time for this," he groaned.

"I've found them!"

"Found what?"

"*Zombies!* I found the bastards! I said I would, and you told me to come back if I did!"

Another exhausted moan. Dwight brought his hands to his face. "Mrs. Hendrickson, it's really, really late." He looked back up at her with pleading eyes. "Why don't you go home and get some rest, yeah? I'm sure you'll forget all of this zombie business in the morning."

"Nonsense!" she said, stomping her foot into the ground. "I have to show you! Everybody in this godforsaken neighborhood thinks I'm losing my mind, but I ain't losing a damned thing! You have to come and see for yourself!"

Dwight heard footsteps coming down the stairs. "Daddy?"

"It's okay Jimmy," he said. "Go on back to bed." He looked at Mrs. Hendrickson and shook his head. "I can't go anywhere right now. Nobody's here to keep an eye on Jimmy."

"Bring him with you!" She smiled at Jimmy. "How would you like to see some zombies, young lad?"

"Daddy says they don't exist."

"Hogwash! Even more reason you should come with me *right now*. You need your eyes opened, the both of you!"

Dwight rubbed his temples and shook his head once more. A sigh of defeat escaped his lips at the realization that Mrs. Hendrickson was adamant about them going with her and wouldn't leave until they agreed. At least it wasn't a school night. Maybe it was better they went with her so he could keep a close eye on her. The last thing Dwight needed was the thought of Mrs. Hendrickson attacking some homeless guy while screaming, "Zombie! Zombie!"

"Fine, we'll go and check it out." He looked at Jimmy. "You okay with going?

Jimmy nodded, slowly.

"It'll be okay," Dwight told him. "Go get your coat and shoes."

"And baseball bats!" Mrs. Hendrickson suggested.

Dwight shook his head. "No bats."

"Fine, but don't' come cryin' to me when a zombie is munching on your skull."

Another sigh, and Dwight told her to wait while they got ready. When he turned he saw Jimmy wearing his red *Mighty Power Fighters* jacket. The boy shoved his hands into his pockets and looked down at his feet.

"Don't worry," Dwight said. "We're not going to see any zombies, but we're going with Mrs. Hendrickson so she doesn't do anything foolish."

"I'm scared."

"There's no need." He looked at the jacket and smiled. "Be brave, like a *Mighty Power Fighter*. Zombies wouldn't scare them, now would they?"

A grin spread across Jimmy's little face. "Nothing scares the *Mighty Power Fighters*."

Dwight laughed and rubbed Jimmy's hair. "Of course not. They're fearless, just like you."

When they were ready, Dwight opened the door and the two of them followed Mrs. Hendrickson as she marched through the neighborhood like a proud general going to war. Dwight walked with his hands in his pockets while randomly mumbling to himself under his breath. Jimmy asked him a few times what he was saying, but he just shook him off.

"You guys better keep up!" Mrs. Hendrickson said.

Dwight grumbled and shook his head.

"Dad, do you really think we'll see zombies?"

He didn't answer, patting Jimmy on the shoulder and giving him a smile, saying that everything was going to be okay without words.

They continued to walk for blocks while the sky above grew dark. It seemed like they were the only ones out, which was kind of eerie. It had all of the right ingredients for a classic horror movie—a crazed woman leading a father and son through an abandoned neighborhood to face the terror lurking somewhere in the shadows. Were there really zombies? Could that be possible? Dwight shook his head and silently scolded himself for even considering such a ludicrous thought. They were only humoring Mrs. Hendrickson and keeping an eye on her.

They finally came to a halt when Mrs. Hendrickson pointed to the neighborhood park in front of them. "There! They're over there!"

It took Dwight a moment to figure out what she was pointing at, and then he saw the two teenagers sitting on swings. They were pale and skinny, but they certainly weren't zombies...though they did appear to be a bit out of sorts. The one on the right gazed up at the sky while dragging his feet along the gravel. The boy on the left stared down at the ground, wiping his nose every now and then with his sleeve. Their resemblance to Sammie hit him almost instantly, and at that point he wished they really *were* zombies. The truth of it was worse. He felt something wrap around him, and when he looked down he saw that it was Jimmy hugging him from behind.

Mrs. Hendrickson placed her bony hands around her mouth, forming a cup. "We know what you are! You ain't fooling us for a second! You go away now, you no good zombies! You won't be eating *my* brains tonight, that's for damn sure!"

The two stoned teenagers slowly looked up and blinked, then began to laugh hysterically. One of the kids even slid out of his swing and fell to the ground, holding his knees, saliva dripping from his mouth with each guffaw. The other covered his eyes, drool clinging to his lips as he snickered.

Dwight tapped Mrs. Hendrickson on the shoulder. "I think it's time that we go now."

"Go? I told you they're zombies! We have to do something!"

"They're not going to hurt anybody tonight. Really, we need to leave." He took her by the hand and started to walk away from the park, with Jimmy following. Mrs. Hendrickson protested, but Dwight assured her that it would be okay and that he would call somebody when he got home. She wouldn't give up on the zombie angle, but Dwight was too drained to explain what they really were.

When they returned, Dwight told Jimmy to go on inside while he took Mrs. Hendrickson back to her house.

"I can find my own damn house, thank you very much," she spat.

"Humor me, and let me walk you home."

Along the way, Mrs. Hendrickson kept going on about how they needed to do something before the zombies attacked the neighborhood, and again Dwight told her that he would take care of it. She needed to go home where it was safe, he explained. He kept repeating this all the way to her house. When she finally went inside he headed home, certain she would stay put.

He stood in his darkened living room, staring out the window as if the trees outside would offer some sort of an answer. He didn't know what to do. He supposed he should call the police and let them know that drugged-out teens were hanging around the neighborhood. He also supposed he should figure out what to do about Mrs. Hendrickson, although he didn't know any of her relatives that he could call. Her delusions were becoming worse, and he was positive the day would come when she'd either hurt herself or someone else.

Dwight didn't do anything but stand in a silent trance.

"Dad," he heard Jimmy say. He didn't turn around. Even when his son was standing right by his side, he didn't move. "Dad, are they really zombies?"

"I guess in a way they are," Dwight whispered. He wished they never followed Mrs. Hendrickson to that godforsaken park. It brought back too many bad memories and feelings.

Jimmy hugged him. "They're nothing but dead things, Dad. Don't worry, I'll protect you from them."

Dwight smiled for the first time that night. A feeling washed over him, one he wished would never disappear.

DEAD THINGS

Michael Crane *is the sick and twisted author of* Lessons and Other Morbid Drabbles, In Decline *(stories), and* A Gnome Problem *(a novelette). He went to Columbia College Chicago where he earned a BA in Fiction Writing. He currently lives in Illinois where he continues to write and drink way too many Red Bulls.*

DOES LAURA LIKE ELEPHANTS?

by Steven Pirie

It's late Friday evening in the pub, and Laura's in her wheelchair too close to the fire in the hearth. The heat burns her leg and stings tears under her eyelids. Her world spins sideways when her head lolls to her shoulder. She feels spittle on her chin, and phlegm in her throat. She gags, but no one notices. She's been gagging all evening, but Pete and the others are good at not noticing. And her thighs are still chaffed from Pete fucking her earlier. Or was it Don? Since the *incident*, anybody could be fucking her and she'd not know.

And Pete says: "I hear there's a two-for-one offer on entrance to the zoo."

"I'm not surprised," says Maureen. "The zoo's crap. I've been, and I counted just the one bored-looking penguin last time."

"They have got a new elephant," says Don.

Pete grins. "A new *old* elephant. I heard it was one Whipsnade didn't want any more. Maybe it was a defective one."

"Laura used to like the elephants," says Don. He sighs. "And the lemurs."

They turn toward Laura, and she twitches in her wheelchair, feeling their stares upon her as harsh as any fire in the hearth. She feels her eyeballs flicking in their sockets.

Maureen laughs. "Now she can't tell them apart, eh?" She leans forward, turning Laura's ear toward her. Laura's world spins once more. "Do you know the difference between an elephant and a lemur, Laura?" She taps Laura's head, and inside the sound booms like in an empty chamber. "Is it the sort of thing you think about alone in there all day?"

"Don't," says Don. "You shouldn't be laughing at Laura."

"Then again," says Maureen, "maybe we should go to the zoo, Pete. You could take Laura. It'll be nice for her to be amongst the moth-eaten animals, seeing as she's defective herself. It'll be like she's with equals. Maybe you can swap her for a smarter looking chimp when no one's looking."

Don downs his pint. "That's not fair," he says. His face has reddened. "Laura can't help the way she is, and you shouldn't be mocking her."

"It's true Laura did like animals, though," says Pete. "Back when she was compos mentis, I mean, back before the *incident*. Perhaps a day out in the fresh air will do her some good."

"Then it's settled," says Maureen. "Tomorrow, after lunch, we'll all have an afternoon at the zoo, and if we can tell Laura apart from the gibbons, *intellectually*, then the coffees are on me."

* * *

Later, back home, it's cold and dark downstairs alone. Laura can't shiver, not since her brain and muscle and sinew all but parted company, and when Pete's pissed-up, when he can't be bothered carrying her upstairs to bed, he leaves her in the wheelchair downstairs in the corner by the fish tank. It's safer that way, he says, in case he falls backward on the stairs. As if Laura would mind snapping her neck as she tumbled. Sometimes he leaves her down when Maureen slips away from Don and comes back for a nightcap.

Laura knows each fish by name; even the dead ones Pete forgets to flush. The tank heater rumbles and gurgles, and the bubbles from the fish-shit encrusted diver ripple dull rainbows on the living room ceiling. The shifting colours are hypnotic. Beyond the glass the fish bob aimlessly, sluggish and directionless like the stray thoughts in Laura's head.

Did she ever like elephants? She doesn't think so. But then, she's not sure it's *she* who stinks of puke and urine since Pete's not bothered changing her *bag* since lunch time. When you're not sure of *that*, how can you be sure of anything?

The tank thermostat trips and the heater switches off. The fish shift, startled by the silence, like they do the dozen times an hour the heater starts and stops. And somewhere, in the dark depths of Laura's brain, as if triggered by the sudden quiet, a neuron fires. A second answers it, and a third, and Laura knows there'll be a storm soon. It's the only way her mind works these days, by unleashing raging torrents of activity. It's only by letting axons burn freely can she think.

Do I like elephants? she asks herself.

DOES LAURA LIKE ELEPHANTS?

She feels lightning streak in her head and hears the rush of wind in her ears. The colours on the ceiling deepen to a painful hue. A dull ache grows behind her eyes. Her limbs don't move, yet in her mind she sees them thrashing against her wheelchair. But by morning she'll know the answer. She'll know if she likes elephants, and in some small way that's one more step toward knowing herself once more.

And lemurs, she adds, what about lemurs?

* * *

It's warm, Saturday morning. Laura's slumped in her wheelchair outside in the garden to the rear by the bins. *Out of the way*, Pete says, while he trundles the Vax over the carpet by the fish tank. The carpet by the fish tank is threadbare by Pete's Vax.

Don's here. Laura knows his cheap aftershave. It goes everywhere Don goes and lingers where he's been. Sometimes, during the neuron storms, Laura thinks she smells it on her blouse.

"Sorry about last night," Don says. He leans inward to fuss with Laura's blanket and pillow. "Maureen's a right arsehole when she's pissed. We all have our own ways of dealing with the aftermath of the *incident*, and Maureen's is to be brash and mocking. She doesn't really mean it. I'll bet she's sorry this morning."

Don lifts Laura's chin with a finger. His skin is warm and firm against her cheek. Laura shudders; it's a caring touch where Pete's is now only a carer's. She knows there's a subtle difference.

Don stares down into her eyes. He looks tired, with more crow's feet than Laura remembers. But Don's eyes are ocean deep, and the flecks of orange in his pupils add fire to his gaze. Maureen and Pete won't look into her eyes like that. Perhaps they're afraid they might somehow be drawn in, to swap places, and maybe rightly so considering none of them truly understand the *incident*.

"Don't you go worrying," says Don. "It will work out in the end."

He smoothes a fold in Laura's dress, and for a moment his fingers brush and linger against her breast below. She wears the pink bra, delicate and *feminine*, not like the great ship-building plates Maureen wears. Laura's bra is lacy and sheer, so much that a hint of nipple pokes through, hardening against Don's knuckle. He turns his finger in small circles against the nub.

67

Laura sees Don's face flush. "Yeah, well, I'd better go." Don stands, panting, awkward. He covers his groin with his left hand. "Maureen expects us at the zoo, and you know what she's like when she expects something. I'll see you later."

Laura wants to cry out to him: "Don't leave."

In her mind she reaches out. But what good are arms that don't rise, hands that won't grasp, lips that can't kiss?

Laura wants to weep.

*　*　*

It's a small zoo. Its paths are hilly and broken, and Don pants as he shoves Laura's wheelchair around the potholes. Laura feels his breath, rhythmically warm and cold against the nape of her neck. Even as the neuron storm of the night before fades, Laura remembers she's felt his breath on her neck like that before.

"It's bloody worse than I remember," says Maureen. "It's all weeds and a few motley wildebeest. Those tortoises haven't moved since the last time I was here."

Pete grips Maureen playfully by the earlobe. She yells and falls into him, and the two fumble against each other. Even Laura notices their embrace lasts longer than it need do. Behind her, she *feels* Don look away.

"Stop moaning," says Pete. "We're doing the zoo even if I have to lead you around it by the ear."

"It won't take long," says Maureen. "Most of the animals have gone anyway."

"Still, it's fresh air for Laura," says Don. "It'll do her good. The trip's for Laura's benefit don't forget."

They walk under a rusted monorail overtaken by weeds, a relic from a time when the zoo held grander thoughts. Beyond that the trees grow unchecked, arching into each other across the path. Through this darkened, tangled canopy the branches hang down like the snapped synapses in Laura's brain. Laura stiffens; she's suddenly unsure whether she's inside or outside her head. It panics her. It's like the *incident* all over again. She's not sure she can live through another *incident*.

"Follow the signs," says Pete. "Elephants, this way."

"Elephant," says Maureen. "Just the one. I read in this morning's paper Whipsnade's reject went tusks-up last Thursday."

DOES LAURA LIKE ELEPHANTS?

"Poor bugger," says Don.

"Ah, here we are; Elephant House and Coffee Shop," says Pete. "Who's for cappuccinos?"

"And a cake for me," says Maureen.

Don nods. "Pick a table near the fence, and I'll nip in for the coffees."

Laura hears in colors. She feels in sounds. Since the *incident*, it's a forced synaesthesia that most people would fear. But when the neuron storms fade Laura will grasp at any sense that comes her way however jumbled.

She *feels* the lumbering thud of the one good elephant beyond the electrified fence, *hears* the drying mud clinging to its skin. She *smells* its bulk, and *tastes* the cleaving of the air by its trunk.

Ah, yes, elephant, she thinks, *I remember elephants. But do I like them?*

"When are you going to tell Don?" says Pete.

Maureen shifts uneasily in her seat. "We've been through this. I'm not moving in with you while *she's* there. It'll be too weird."

Across time and space, the elephant sings to Laura. Its song is flat and endless like the Savannah. Where it lilts, it does so sifting over memories of the herd, filled with dirge and eulogy to bleached white bones abandoned in the scrub. Laura drinks its soul and shudders at the bitter taste.

"Well, there might be some news on that," says Pete.

"Oh?"

"I got a letter from Social Services. They tell me there'll be a place soon for Laura at the Twilight Years Care Home, seeing as she's worsening."

Maureen laughs. "It's not really called that, is it?"

"Something like it."

"And is she worsening?"

"Nah, but I thought it couldn't harm to say so."

Laura soars with the elephant's soul above the African plains. Wind and sand sting her cheek. Over leaping gazelles and lumbering buffalo they fly. And the land is forever and the warmth never ending. They see elephants in the distance, dark shapes plodding-slow, as only elephants can be.

These are your kin? thinks Laura. She knows the answer; she tastes it in the elephant's thudding heart. *Then this is where you should be, not trapped here alone in such dreadful captivity.*

"Tell Don, and then come over tonight," says Pete. "We can put Laura downstairs out of the way until whoever it is pegs it at Twilight Years. Come over; I'm tired of shagging Laura. It's like poking a bean bag."

Maureen frowns. *"I'm tired of fucking a cabbage* is not the basis for ours to be a good relationship."

"You know what I mean." Pete takes her hand. "It's you I want."

"Look, Don's on his way back," says Maureen. "I'll slip out tonight and we'll talk about it, right?"

Alone in such dreadful captivity, Laura repeats. *Just like me.*

* * *

There's a storm Saturday night. Laura is locked in the conservatory. The air is stuffy and warm, and sickly with the aroma of scented candles seeping in through the ill-fitting French doors. There was a time, Laura thinks, back when she knew about lemurs and elephants, when Pete would put scented candles out for her. Now he lolls about drinking beer and farting as if she's not there.

Lightning flashes beyond the glass windows. It burns an image onto Laura's eyelids—the tangle of trees in the woods beyond the garden fence. She holds it there, tracing the detail of each branch, each twig delicately connected to its neighbor, held frozen in an instant of time. In her mind, Laura fingers the tree bark down to the wet earth below; loses herself in the nooks and ridges of the wood; invades these miniature worlds of grubs and insects and life and death.

Laura pauses, suddenly afraid. It's in contemplating such intricacies of the world that brought on the *incident*. It was then that the universe rushed into her head. Human brains weren't made to understand entire universes. It was little wonder veins popped.

Laura reins her thoughts, pushing them back outward into the meaningless macro world of Pete and Maureen and candles, and of Don sitting at home blissfully unaware of all of them. Rain bangs down upon the conservatory roof. It's insistent, like Pete's grunts and Maureen's groans from the living room floor. She sees the rise and fall of Pete's buttocks reflected in the conservatory window; up and down like two pale, nervous ghosts.

Laura sighs.

DOES LAURA LIKE ELEPHANTS?

Life moves on.

Laura wonders whether it's time she did so too.

* * *

The pub does a fine Sunday Lunch. Sunday lunch and darts at the pub was always something of a ritual back before the *incident*. Laura's in her chair, tucked in the corner under the rubber plant. Her head is forward, her chin resting on her chest like she's nodded off asleep. She sees Pete's fingers trace circles on Maureen's thigh beneath the table. Occasionally Maureen reaches down and grips his hard-on just to keep him going.

"Did you see Jonathon Ross last night?" says Don.

"Nah," says Pete, "I had other things to do." He winces as Maureen glares at him and grips him harder below.

"He had that bloke who does the stunts as a guest. You know, the *hangs-upside-down-and-doesn't-eat-and-drink-for-a-month* bloke. It's bloody marvellous how he went for a month without sustenance."

"That's all trickery," says Pete. "I bet he took water through a straw in his arse or something."

Maureen spills her beer. "That would be a good trick in itself."

"Besides," says Pete, "Why bother?"

Laura feels the spin of the world beneath her feet. The rumble of the planet through space dislodges dust in her head. Beyond that, she feels the grinding of the galaxy against the interstellar clouds. It's a journey, she thinks; all of them embarked upon a journey they can't get off. All of them locked in a rotating prison without keys.

She explores Death, flitting spirit-like and fey across the old cemetery on London Road. The headstones are old here, chipped and blackened, and strewn with moss. The dead below these slabs have long since accepted their fate. But they still cry out to Laura as she swoops by. Their mews are weak and pitiful. There's no sleep down here, they say, no rest in the dark, damp earth. And the sodden ground tries to suck Laura down. How much easier would it be to let it do so? What's left for her in the physical world, after all?

"It's an endurance thing, I suppose," says Maureen. "Man against Nature, and all that."

"What's bloody natural about hanging upside down for a month?" says Pete.

Maureen grins. "I don't know; ask bats."

Laura feels bile rise in her throat. With her head thrown forward and downward like this she's not in the best position to deal with vomiting. She forces her eyeballs upward in their sockets trying to see across to Don, but he's stuck in some stupid conversation. She's not surprised; stupid conversations were always the norm where Pete and Maureen were concerned. Laura's chest hurts, and there are lights behind her eyes. She's all but ready to die. Except there's one more thing she must do.

"I think it's impressive," says Don, "Hanging about like that for an entire month."

Pete shakes his head. "It doesn't matter; it's all a trick."

"It all looked pretty real to me," says Don. "Jonathon Ross said the guy's stunts were *officiated* over."

"Lots of things look real to you, Don," says Pete.

There's a short silence.

"What's that supposed to mean?"

"The thing is, Don," says Pete, "is that Maureen's moving in with me."

Don looks on open mouthed and wide eyed. Laura slumps further forward in her chair. She's choking and can't breathe. There are shooting pains in her left arm. She reaches out to Don across time and space, and finds his soul amongst the chaos of the world.

"I'm with you, Don," she says, her voice loud and clear inside Don's head. "I'm with you now and always."

"Well bugger me," says Don.

* * *

Laura's buried on Thursday. It's raining, and Pete's worried his suit will get wet. Maureen's not there. She says she *doesn't do* funerals, not unless it's *close*. Don's there. He stands across from Pete, his eyes hidden behind darkened glasses. The opened grave is a chasm between them, a divide that sets them a world away from each other, yet somehow joined by Laura lying between them.

"She's better off," says Pete. "She died back in January with the apoplexy."

Don nods. He hesitates to speak. When he does so, his voice is thin, quiet, and unsure. "I touched her soul, you know." Don studies Pete's face. There's no hint of understanding. But then, even Don can't really fathom what truly went on with the *incident*. "Or, perhaps Laura found mine. It's the same thing. We were two free spirits trying to make sense of the world when our worlds met."

"You were having an affair?"

Don nods again. "I suppose there's no reason to hide it now. You'll not understand, and if you do you'll not believe me. But our souls merged that night, and it was so intense it all but broke Laura's body. That was the *incident*. It wasn't madness that took her, or the depression, or the alcohol, or the popped veins in her head, rather she bore the brunt of our fusion and pulled away. Maybe she did so to save me, I don't know. It's a noble thought I like to carry with me. It's a terrible thought I have to live with."

Pete shakes his head slowly and turns away. What he's thinking, he doesn't say. Don wonders if that's part of the reason Laura never found *his* soul.

Don stays by the graveside, watching as Pete ambles down the damp pathway to the waiting limousine. When he nears the cemetery gates Pete turns back.

"Hey, Don," he calls. "You do know you're as fucked up as she was?"

*   *   *

A month goes by. Don's comfortable with Laura's passing. Each day he was forced to look upon her in that vegetative state was a torment on him. And he's fine with Maureen washing Pete's shirts. The bitter days when he thinks they deserve each other are growing fewer.

But his head feels *different*, that's the curious thing. Don's lost count of the times he's wandered trance like only to wake at one or other of Laura's favourite haunts—the *Mystical Shop* on King's Road, the *Spiritual Library* on Faulkner Street, the pagan stone hidden away down Duke's Close—places they'd say only the two of them knew about, and where they'd meet secretly when for all they knew Pete was busy seeing Maureen.

Don's at the zoo. He sits alone, staring in at the elephant being hosed and brushed by its keeper. It's tranquil, here, a place where Don can sift through memories of Laura.

He smiles, thinking how they'd argue playfully about her passion with the mystical. *Mumbo jumbo*, he'd call it, and she'd wrestle him to the grass, pin down his arms and kiss his mouth.

73

There's more to life than meets the eye, she'd say, and Don would roll her over and wish they were naked.

In the depths of his mind, he feels Laura stir. She pushes a thought against him and Don resists at first but then welcomes it. There's pain above his eyes. For all he knows, it could be veins popping in his head.

"Everything's connected, Don," says Laura. "Everything touches everything else on a fundamental level. It's all one if we just reach out to each other."

"I don't understand," says Don.

"It doesn't matter. Take my hand. Come with me."

Together they soar high above the zoo. The wind is in their hair, the damp air in their faces.

"Do you like elephants?" says Don.

"I do, Don, and I love lemurs."

Laura pauses. At last she's whole again. Their two spirits entwine.

"But most of all I love life…and you."

Steven Pirie *lives in Liverpool, UK, with his wife and son. His fiction has appeared in magazines and anthologies around the world. His comic fantasy novel,* Digging up Donald, *published by Immanion Press in 2004 and again in 2007, has attracted excellent reviews. A new novel,* Burying Brian, *was published also by Immanion Press in December 2010.*

Steve's website is: www.stevenpirie.com

DOES LAURA LIKE ELEPHANTS?

39 DAYS

by Robert J. Duperre

August 18th

Waves crashed against the side of the building. To Angela it sounded like the rocky coast of Maine. She leaned over the roof and glanced down. The water smacked against the building again and flowed around it. She swore she could see formless black splotches beneath the surface and immediately imagined a capsized oil tanker dumping gallon after gallon of crude into the ocean.

"How high is it now?" asked Tommy.

She furrowed her brow and counted the windows above the water line. "Fourth floor," she said, "almost to the fifth."

"Shit. That's higher than yesterday."

A stout wind hit her from the rear, momentarily lifting her knees from the concrete. Her hair stood straight out, hovering over the angry sea below. With a yelp she gripped tight to the railing and spun around, wedging her butt in the crook between the partition and the floor. Tommy hurried over to her, eyes wide with panic.

"You okay?" he asked.

Angela nodded.

Tommy slumped beside her. The wind died down. He crawled to the center of the roof, rummaged through his backpack, and brought back a handful of snacks.

"You hungry?"

"Sure."

They sat there together, munching on Nilla Wafers and staring at the gray and ominous sky. A few drops of rain began to fall.

They burned.

August 20th

A helicopter soared overhead. It landed on the building three down from where Angela and Tommy had been trapped. The few people on the roof rushed it and men in fatigues ushered them aboard. The helicopter rose again and disappeared over the horizon.

"How many's that now?" asked Angela.

"Fifteen over the last week," Tommy replied. "Looks like they're working their way toward us. Might only be a few days 'till it's our turn."

Angela grunted. "Good. I'm getting tired of sitting around doing nothing."

She stood up and cracked her back. For the first time in a week the sun poked its warming face through the clouds. She bathed in its heat and spread out her arms. Lesions covered her skin, the result of not getting into the complex in time when the poisoned rains fell. Even their tent hadn't been spared – its canvas hide was peppered with black marks and tiny holes. It was better than nothing, however. A headache spiked behind her eyes. She crawled inside.

The interior of the tent was hot, and she found it hard to breathe. She tried to get comfortable, flapping her sleeping bag in an attempt to alleviate the humid miasma that had gathered in its cloth cocoon. Nothing seemed to help. It was still hotter than hell.

With a sigh she crawled back out of the tent, towing the sleeping bag behind her, and spread it out on the roof. She lay down on it and curled into a ball, squeezing her eyes shut against the intense brightness of the outside world. She felt Tommy kneel beside her.

"You want some company?" he asked.

Angela grunted in affirmation.

Tommy slid in behind her and wrapped his arm around her midsection. He wedged his forearm into the underside of her breasts. She felt his breath against the back of her neck while her skin tingled with the sun's rays.

For the first time since the whole mess started Angela smiled and allowed the sound of the crashing waves to usher her off to sleep.

August 25th

It had been four days since the last chopper came around, and Angela started to get nervous. At least the sun had stayed out. It made the days scorching, especially on the roof's harsh concrete, but by the middle of the night, when the air cooled to almost arctic temperatures, she wished for the heat to return. *Damned either way,* she thought.

She made her way to the edge of the roof and gazed across the watery landscape. Hartford had become one with the ocean. That ocean rose every day, approaching their sanctuary with ever-greedy fingers. Luckily for her and Tommy, they lived in one of the taller apartment complexes on the east end of the city. The water was still a good sixty feet from overtaking them. That gave them time, at least.

But that time was running out.

"Yo, Ang!" a faint voice called out to her.

She turned around. On the roof of the apartment building to the west stood Rachid and Roberta Freeman, surrounded by their four children and Dexter McCutchens. They waved at her and held up a handwritten sign. *Want to play a game?* it read.

Tommy chuckled from behind her. "Checkers again?" he asked.

Angela bent over, grabbed the wax board they'd been using to communicate with those stranded on the other roof for the last couple of weeks, and scribbled *Sure thing, your move* in large letters. She held it up and watched as little Jermaine Freeman smiled. Even from a distance, she could see the whites of his teeth.

They played for a few hours, until the sun began dipping over the horizon. When it became impossible to see, Angela and Tommy simply packed up their cheap checkerboard and tossed it into the tent. "See you tomorrow!" screamed Tommy. They could barely hear when their far-away friends returned the sentiment.

They crawled into their sleeping bag as the night began its assault of frigid air. Tommy's body radiated heat, he smelled of sweet body odor, and for not the first time she wondered why it had taken an asteroid plummeting into the Pacific Ocean for them to so much as speak to each other.

August 30th

At first when she heard the sound, Angela assumed it was her stomach rumbling again. She lifted her head and stared at the sky. The moon shone down on her with its bluish glow, but she noticed clouds beginning to roll in once more. *Damn*, she thought. *Not more rain.* They couldn't afford to spend time indoors, not with the possibility of rescue. If the helicopters showed up again, they had to be out and ready.

The sound intensified, shaking her to the core, and she rose to her feet, nudging Tommy awake in the process. He stirred and sat up.

"What's going on?"

"Helicopters, I think."

"At night?"

"I know. Weird."

A spotlight appeared in the distance. It was low, just barely skimming the surface of the water as it progressed from rooftop to rooftop. The tides had risen dramatically of late, and now was only ten feet from overtaking them.

The helicopter hovered over a building. She couldn't tell exactly how far away they were in the dark, but it had to be close. She could hear muffled shouts and a bustle of activity. Soon more voices joined in. Their tone seemed joyous.

The Freemans yelled from their distant perch. "Is it another?" the father's voice asked, small as a mouse's.

"It is!" screamed Tommy.

Angela started jumping up and down, bellowing as loud as she could. "Over here! We're over here! Don't leave us!" Tommy joined in. Even together, their yells seemed to die inches in front of their faces.

The helicopter swerved around, its spinning blades beating a drumbeat of salvation. The spotlight pointed in their direction. It moved forward, approaching them, so close the wind from its rotors blew Angela's hair from her face.

It drifted slowly across the rippling water. A strange, violet glow appeared beneath it, like millions of fireflies below the surface. Angela's breath caught in her throat. The ocean rose up a giant hand that wrapped itself around the helicopter's frame. The blades cut through the water, and it seemed to scream. Then, quick as a blink, it was forced into the water nose-first. The rotors snapped. Angela felt a rush of air against her cheek. Quick as she could she threw her arm around Tommy and forced him to the ground. Shrapnel rained around them. Frightened screams echoed over the waves. Angela squeezed her eyes shut. She felt Tommy shudder and cry out.

This was it. She knew it.

Tears ran down her cheeks in torrents.

September 1st

Angela held Tommy close. A light drizzle started to fall, biting her flesh but not enough to make her move. She shivered in the cold breeze and held her breath. But for the waves, all was silent.

After a while she lifted her head. A gray haze dulled everything. She stood up and looked behind her. The Freemans were still huddled together on the roof of their building. None looked up at her, even when she called out to them. Dexter McCutchens was nowhere to be seen.

Water trickled over the retaining wall. She drifted to the side of the building, cringed, and looked down. The level had risen overnight and the sea was choppy. Waves collided with the walls and flowed into the smashed windows on the level just below. She lifted her gaze, following the horizon line, taking in the new, watery world. Distant skyscrapers jutted from the sea as it slowly swallowed everything. And there were twinkling lights in the water now, the same sort of lights that came before the helicopter had been taken under the previous evening. She thought of those trapped inside the hulk of steel as it plunged beneath the ocean surface. Were they devoured by whatever it was that had taken them? Did they drown? In either case it seemed a horrible way to go.

Thoughts of her family entered her mind, and Angela crumpled. She writhed on the concrete while acid rain washed over her. Had her mother and father succumbed to the same fate as those in the chopper? When the oceans rose, had their house in the Cape been among the first to go? Were they dead? Were they suffering? Or had they found their own rooftop? Were they, like Angela, now hovering perilously close to the edge, surviving day-by-day, and waiting, just waiting, for the water to flood their sanctuary and bring them to the hungry mouths of whatever lay just beneath the surface?

She cried, long and hard. Her lungs and throat burned. She bellowed until she couldn't any longer and then lay there, shaking and whimpering, ready to give up.

A gentle hand touched her shoulder. Angela looked up through moist eyes. It was Tommy. Of course it was. He wore a half-smile on his face and gazed down at her with affection. She brought her hand up and touched his cheek. It was soft, despite lumps of irritation where the rain had hit it. He leaned in and planted his lips on hers. She went with it, running her tongue over his mouth, opening wide, taking in all the comfort he had to offer.

Tommy lifted her up and brought her to the tent. He placed her inside, sealed the flap, and gradually undressed her. His mouth found her again, moved from her lips to neck to breasts to belly, placing gentle pecks wherever the burning rain had left its mark.

They made love for the first time in the depressing, soggy haze of morning. There was no crying out in pleasure for either of them. No moans of satisfaction left their throats. There were only soft sighs in the darkness of the tent, moving in tune with the crashing waves, using each other's bodies for solace as if the gyrations could shake away the sorrow that had swallowed all hope.

September 8th

Overnight, the Freemans disappeared. Angela kept vigil on the side closest to their building, hoping they would appear from inside, hold up a sign, and tell them all was fine.

It never happened. They were simply…gone.

Angela's stomach rumbled. She doubled over in pain. Over the last few days, they'd run out of food and water. The last of the supplies Tommy had retrieved from the upper floors before they became submerged were gone. They'd thought they had plenty, surely enough to get by until help arrived. Now all they had to sustain themselves were the pigeons that sometimes landed on the roof. But getting their hands on the birds proved a tedious task, at best. They'd only caught three over the last seven days, and had to tear them apart with bare hands and eat them raw. At first Angela thought she couldn't do it. Her savage hunger won out, however, and the second time she dove into the bloody meal like a starving lioness.

The worst, however, was the lack of water. They dared not drink the ocean water, even if they'd had the bravery to get close enough to obtain some. So they settled on gathering rainwater and drinking that. It was murky in their canteens and stung going down. Often they vomited after consuming it. But the body required water, and it was their only choice, so they dealt with it as best they could.

The ocean lights had begun to multiply, as well. They floated around the building like strings of Christmas lights, illuminating the evenings and casting a dull glow during the day. Angela decided that under different circumstances she might have found them pretty. The question of where they'd come from was the furthest thing from her mind.

To pass the time, she and Tommy made love. Every day, three times or more. The act allowed them at least a few fleeting moments of normalcy, of comfort. They would lay in each others' arms afterward, shielded by their rapidly deteriorating tent, and talk about what they'd do when the world returned to normal. Not that either of them believed this would happen. Angela, for her part, was resigned to her eventual fate. Her only wish was to go on for one more day, despite the pain.

She was stubborn like that.

September 12th

"We need something to eat," said Tommy. "We need it now."

"I know," Angela replied, defeated. "But how are we gonna get some?"

The pigeons had ceased landing on the roof; like the Freemans, they seemed to have vanished. Even the seagulls, which she'd often noticed flocking around the tops of the taller skyscrapers as if they feared getting too close to the rising tides, were gone. It seemed the whole of the earth above the surface of the ocean had ceased to exist. For a moment Angela thought she and Tommy might be the last humans alive. She shuddered and forced that assumption from her mind.

"We can get some canned goods from the apartments," said Tommy. "There was still a bunch of stuff in there before they flooded. Even bottled water. It should still be fine."

"But we already talked about that. It...it's under water."

"I know. But heck, I can swim."

"But..."

Tommy's brow creased. His eyes looked tired. "There's no other choice, Ang. It's either that or starve."

They made their way down the stairs. At least the flooding hadn't reached that high yet. It wasn't until they reached the top floor that they saw the water. It glistened in the weak light coming from the stairwell, but still appeared brown and dirty. Tommy plunged in. It came up to his waist. Angela followed. The water was cold. Goosebumps rose on her flesh.

They waded down the hallway until they reached apartment 14C. It was the old Beaulieu place, a nice older couple who'd fled, along with most of the city, when news of the impending tides spread. At the time, Angela had wanted to join them. It was Tommy, who lived in the apartment opposite hers, who came up with the idea to take refuge on the roof. *It takes hours to reach the*

Green Mountains, he'd said. *And that's with no traffic. With everyone trying to reach higher ground, we'd be lucky to get there before the water gets us. Our best bet is to stay here and wait for help to come.*

They entered the apartment. Magazines and other detritus floated past them. Tommy led Angela to the kitchen. The countertops were just above the waterline, islands of white marble resting in a brown sea.

"I'm going under," Tommy said.

Angela hopped from foot to foot, her body growing numb in the cold water. "You need help?"

"I'll be fine."

Tommy dove beneath the surface. The water was so murky Angela couldn't see any part of him when he submerged. Air bubbles popped in his place. Something brushed against her leg and she jumped, hoping beyond hope it was only Tommy as he rummaged through the lower cabinets.

A minute later he reemerged. He held in his arms a stack of canned vegetables. He placed them on the counter and winked at her.

"See, told you," he said. "And I think I felt a case of bottled water down there, too. I'll be right back."

With another deep breath, Tommy plunged back into the murk. Angela took a garbage bag from the shelves to her rear and loaded it with cans. Once more Tommy brushed her leg, only she didn't jump this time. She giggled a bit instead.

"You gotta be more careful!" she yelled at the rising bubbles. "One of these times you'll get a little too close to you-know-where, and then…"

Something caught her eye; flashes, like sparks, coming from the doorway. Slowly she turned her head. Through the opening appeared a clump of shimmering lights. It moved gradually, gracefully, like liquid within liquid, coming toward them. Angela backed up a step.

"Uh, Tommy?" She swallowed a lump, tried to call for him again, and couldn't. Fear choked her.

Tommy hadn't come up.

In a panic, she thrust her arms into the water. Her hands searched blindly for him, but came away with nothing. A quick glance told her the approaching tube of sludge and light was halfway across the kitchen. She searched harder. Her foot caught on something, and she fell forward. Her face splashed below the surface. Stinging salt water ran down her throat. She thrashed around, trying to regain her footing.

"Ang, what's wrong?"

Angela stopped her flaying and looked at the voice. Tommy stood before her, away from the counter, on the other side of the room. He held up a twelve-pack of Evian with his right hand, oblivious to the thing coming up behind him.

She opened her mouth to speak, but no words came out.

"Did I scare you? Sorry. I thought it'd be a good joke to swim around you. You know, surprise you a little. I guess it was a stupid idea."

The thing in the water started to encircle him. Tommy never saw it. He simply stared at Angela with a look of concern in his eyes. It wasn't until the thing's flashing, ethereal lights floated in front of him that he looked down.

Tommy screamed. A cylinder of brown water rose up and wrapped itself around his chest. One moment he was above water, the next he disappeared. Angela watched with eyes bulging, afraid to move. A frantic pool of air bubbles appeared where Tommy had stood. Then they stopped.

Angela held her breath. All was quiet but for the sway of the water. She inched to the side, along the counter, heading for the door. Her elbow struck an open drawer. She winced but kept on going.

Tommy's head exploded from the water. Angela screamed. He lashed out with his arms like a drowning man. Strange veins of a substance that looked like seaweed clung to him, pulling him back under. He fought against it. The flesh on his neck singed. The brown water around him turned red. The veins then worked their way to his head. His eyes bulged and he offered a gurgling, blood-filled scream before his cheeks caved in. A few more veins pulled off his lower jaw. It sank into the depths.

Angela dashed out of the kitchen fast as she could. The waist-deep water fought against her with nightmarish force. Tears streamed down her cheeks. In a few moments she was out of the apartment and back in the hallway. Still more clumps of shimmering light approached. She turned away and waded toward the stairs. She could feel their slimy fingers on her heels. The roof access door, still open, was only a few feet away.

Gasping and dripping water, she scurried up the stairs and never once looked back. When she got to the roof, she slammed the door shut and slid down it until her wet butt smacked the concrete.

She sat there and cried, with her head in her hands, for hours.

September 15th

It was night. Angela's stomach cramped. She lay on her back in the middle of the roof, staring up at a star-filled sky. She traced lines from one star to another, making pictures in her mind. Every one came out looking like Tommy.

Another pang wrenched her gut, and she moaned. She hadn't eaten in days. The diseased rainwater she drank tore up her insides. Her throat burned with every sip, and when she looked at her reflection in a puddle, she saw her cheeks were pallid and sunken. She looked like a corpse.

Growing bored and depressed, she rolled over and curled into a ball. She needed sleep, though it seemed sleep was all she did. She closed her eyes and hoped the next time she woke up it wouldn't be in the middle of a nightmare.

September 22nd

Dry weather arrived, and when it did, the seas stopped rising. It was only two feet from the top of the apartment building. Every so often, if there was a strong wind, waves would lash over the sides, covering the roof with brown, tainted water.

Not that Angela cared much. She had no food, no water, no hope. She lingered in the same spot for hours, staring at the cracks in the concrete below her. Her lips were dry and split, her body emaciated and dying.

Her eyes started playing tricks on her. As dehydration set in, she began to see ships in the distance; giant sea-faring vessels that towed behind them nets filled with the remains of all the people she'd known. These ships always stayed just beyond the horizon, painted gray against the curve of the earth. To her mind's eyes they were as big as cities.

She should have been frightened, but she wasn't.

Another crack caught her attention, and she watched it.

September 26th

"King me."

Angela placed one checker on another and grinned. "Good job, Tommy," she said. "Why can't I ever beat you?"

"I'm just good," he replied.

She looked in his eyes. They were so kind and loving. She could gaze into them forever.

"So, what're you lovebirds doing?" asked another voice. Angela turned around. It was Rachid Freeman. He sat in a beach chair, bouncing his little daughter in his lap. He smiled, and his white teeth reflected the sunlight. Roberta approached, handed him a glass of iced tea, and squeezed his hand.

"It's so beautiful out today," she said.

"Sure is. Sun's shining, sand's not too hot, water's cool… could be the best day ever."

Angela grinned. She ran her hand through the sand. They were right. It *was* cool. She giggled, thinking herself silly for not noticing before.

"What's so funny?" asked Tommy.

"Oh, nothing," she replied. "I can just be ridiculous, you know?"

They reclined on a towel that hadn't been there a second ago and let the sun warm their flesh. "Can I ask you a question?" asked Tommy.

"Shoot."

"What do you want to do with your life?"

Angela cocked her head. "Do with my life? What kind of question is that?"

"Just curious."

"Oh, well, I don't know, really. Haven't thought about it much. I guess I'd like to have a good job and…" She bit her lip. "No, that's not right. I think, more than anything, I just want to be happy. I want to be in the moment and *live*. I've seen too many folks live like they're scared of life, and I don't want that to be me."

"So, how'll you pull that off?"

Angela flashed Tommy a mischievous grin. "Right now, by beating you into the water."

She stood up without hesitation and took off. Tommy was right behind her. She dashed across the beach as fast as her legs could carry her and then leapt from the rocks. Tucking her knees to her chest, she plunged beneath the water. As it washed over her she felt soothed by its coolness, especially on a day bright as this one. She wanted to bathe in that feeling forever.

She never came back up.

This story originally appeared in Unnatural Disasters, *edited by* **Daniel Pyle**. *To read more about* **Robert Duperre**, *who lives in Connecticut and edited this collection, please visit http://theriftonline.com.*

39 DAYS

THE CANDLE EATERS

by K. Allen Wood

Katie Adams cut a white swath through the dark of the woods, a ghost to all but the dead.

The crisp night air was its own special vintage, and it soothed her lungs as she weaved between the shadows. A soft breeze caressed her with the smells of October: smoldering brush piles; damp, hungry soil; the breath of cold brick chimneys just waking from their summer-long slumber.

It was her favorite time of the year. The in-between, when the bushes and trees strutted their autumn wardrobes and the wind endlessly whispered the promise of winter.

She emerged from the woods and into the field on the edge of Farmington Circle. The tall grass and weeds whipped across her thighs as she ran toward the small isolated community of Bridgetown Pines.

As she reached the sidewalk, she slowed and caught her breath. She plucked a few sticky burrs from the tattered sheets that made up her ghostly costume and cast them away. Under the canopy of oaks that lined the street, Katie let the beauty of twilight calm her. Like a cleansing rain, the night descended and washed away her loneliness, the anger she harbored toward her mother, and the fear of what lay ahead now that her father was gone.

Grief and regret were such destructive things, parasitical emotions that feasted upon sorrow and pain. Katie had learned this the hard way, having played host to the vile things for the past six months, worrying over what could have been done differently, words that could have been said more often. But she had found no answers in what *could* have been, only in what *was*. So she'd fought back, fought hard, and though her battle was yet won, though she still struggled with the pain and anger and despair, she had a stranglehold on her suffering.

And she wasn't letting go.

Her mother, on the other hand, had given up, given in to the crippling heartache that weighed down upon them both. Katie felt as though she'd shed more tears for the metaphorical loss of her mother than for the real, knife-to-the-heart passing of her father.

Tonight, though, this final October night, she would let it all go, for however brief a moment. Tonight she would once again embrace the wonders of childhood.

For some reason, however, as she continued down the street, her empty pillowcase swinging at her side, Katie had the strange feeling that something was amiss, as if the shadows held secrets best left in the dark. The neighborhood beyond was dead calm, as always; the lawns and shrubbery immaculately groomed and swaying gently in the breeze, but somehow...wrong. The knotted fingers of the trees seemed to loom a bit closer. The symphony of night sounds—insects, birds, small animals rustling in the leaves—was hushed.

Goose bumps prickled her skin. She picked up her pace.

She tried to push her unease aside, ascribe it to overactive imagination, but the feeling dogged her all the way to 18 Farmington Circle, where it vanished like morning mist.

Katie skipped up the driveway—perhaps a little faster than normal—and onto the cobblestone path leading to the side door. Twin wicker chairs sat empty on the wooden patio, a deck of cards splayed on the table between them as if ghosts were enjoying an evening game of Rummy. On the door before her hung a WELCOME sign haloed by an autumnal wreath, its faux berries like clusters of dark beady eyes. Under their scrutinizing gaze, she rang the doorbell.

She glanced over her shoulder, saw nothing out of the ordinary, and wondered what could have made her feel as though something lurked among the shadows. *Knowing the truth of things*, she supposed, coming to know the reality of the world, the insidious truth that childhood innocence had kept hidden from her for seventeen years, until it was swiftly revealed in the most agonizing of ways. Loved ones didn't live forever; best friends would sometimes become enemies; and worst of all, life had razor-sharp, poison-filled fangs that could pierce the human heart—*her* heart. And Katie knew, looking back the way she'd come, literally and figuratively, that darkness always reigned beyond the light.

It wasn't just *something* that was different. *Everything* was different.

THE CANDLE EATERS

The door opened and the scent of spiced apples washed over her. Katie turned, closed her eyes and breathed it in. It reminded her of home, of sweet hugs and cookies in the oven. It reminded her of better times.

"Katie! Come in, come in." Mrs. Hapler opened the door wide. "Matthew will be right down."

Mrs. Hapler was made of sweetness and joy, the kind of woman you loved within minutes of meeting her, as if you'd known her your whole life. Katie smiled, but before stepping inside, she held out her pillowcase...

"Trick or treat?"

Looking dismayed and out of character, Mrs. Hapler frowned. "Matthew didn't tell you, did he? Never mind. I'm not surprised. Unfortunately, dear, we don't have any candy."

"Well, that's too bad." Katie stepped inside and Mrs. Hapler closed the door behind her. "Trick it is, then. May I borrow a roll of toilet paper?"

Mrs. Hapler laughed, warm and friendly. "Don't you even think about!" She opened the refrigerator and removed a Diet Coke. "We don't usually get trick-or-treaters here—you know how it is—so Harold and I are going out to dinner at Cassandra's and then catching a late movie. If he ever gets out of the shower, that is. Would you like something to drink?"

"No, thank you."

"We bought candy our first year here, and no one came. Can you believe that?"

Katie nodded. Bridgetown Pines hadn't been conceived as a retirement community, but for all intents and purposes it had become one. The average age of its residents was just shy of dead. Few children ventured this far north of the city in hopes of getting a handful of wintergreen mints from a few old curmudgeons. And getting a handful of mints was a best-case scenario. The Haplers were the oddity of the neighborhood, still young and sprightly in their forties. Matt was the only kid on the block.

"Not a single person," Mrs. Hapler continued. She tapped the top of the soda can twice, opened it, and took a sip. "And with that big bowl of candy sitting on the table taunting us—I swear Harold and I gained ten pounds a day until it was all gone." She laughed. "But now with his diabetes and all...well, you understand."

Katie's face must have reflected the sadness she'd not yet found a way to hide when she was reminded of her father's passing, for Mrs. Hapler walked over, wrapped her in a loving embrace, and kissed the top of her head. "I'm sorry, dear. I wasn't thinking."

"It's okay," she said, fighting back tears that threatened to ruin her face paint. "I'm fine."

But she wasn't fine, and she wondered if she ever would be.

Her father had been a lifelong diabetic. Six months ago he'd gone to sleep and never woke up. He just slipped away peacefully in the night. She could still remember the morning, the sun slicing through the gaps in her pink blinds, teasing her with its warmth as her mother's wails promised nothing but cold, cold, cold.

As devastated as Katie had been, the worst part of it all was that she'd lost not only her father, but her mother as well. At least it felt that way. Her mother shut down after her father's death, shut everyone and everything out of her life, and descended into a malignant darkness.

Just as the cold hands of despair were reaching up to pull her down into its black depths, Matt bounded into the room and brought a shining smile to her face—Mrs. Hapler's, too. He howled and snarled behind a rubber wolf-mask, making a real show of it. He wore a red-and-black plaid shirt, sleeves cut at the shoulders, and a black hooded sweatshirt underneath. His jeans were ragged and torn, as if he'd been attacked by one of his toothy brethren. A strip of synthetic wolf-hair, from forehead to shoulder, had been dyed green and hair-sprayed into a spiky spine.

"Nice hair," Katie said.

"It's a *wo*hawk," Matt replied, pausing for dramatic effect. "You see what I did there? A punk-rock werewolf."

He howled again.

"Whatever you say, goofball. Hey, I know! Maybe you should join Team Jacob."

"Maybe I should eat your face," he said, pointing a wobbly, elongated finger at her.

"Matthew," Mrs. Hapler said. "How many times have I told you, we don't eat our guests. Especially the nice ones."

"But that's what werewolves do!"

Mrs. Hapler looked at Katie, feigned a sad, contemplative face, and sighed heavily. "He has a point, you know, and since it is Halloween and all, I guess I'll make an exception. But—" she took another sip of her drink "—if you really must eat her face, please do it outside. I just mopped."

"Thanks, Mom! You're the best."

Katie laughed. They always knew how to make her laugh.

Katie and Matt gathered their things and said their good-byes.

"We'll be home sometime after midnight," said Mrs. Hapler. "You two behave, and be careful. And get me a Tootsie Roll."

Then they were out the door, racing down the street and off into the night. They passed through the same field Katie had come through earlier in the evening, intoxicated by the nostalgic promise of excitement and adventure.

They didn't see the pale-faced children creeping along the tree line.

* * *

Two hours later, with pillowcases full of sweet, sugary booty—Tootsie Pops, Smarties, Kit Kats, Snickers, Milky Ways, and so much more—Katie and Matt entered Bridgetown Pines and turned the corner at the far end of Farmington Circle.

Thick woods flanked both sides of the road, and a scant few streetlights did their futile best to hold back the shadows within. The branches overhead clacked like wind chimes constructed of bones. All around, orange and yellow and red leaves lazily floated to their deaths, soft and peaceful.

Katie shook her head, smiling. "What the hell are we going to do with all this candy?"

"Well, I intend to eat it," Matt said, removing his mask and gloves, the transformation back to human far less dramatic than depicted in movies. His face glistened with sweat. "I'm crazy like that."

Katie had a witty comeback lined up, something about agreeing that he was crazy, but the words were swept away in a whirlwind of chatter that exploded within her head, suddenly, painfully, as if she had become hardwired into every cellular network in the world—and everyone was shouting. Her knees buckled.

Matt dropped his pillowcase, reached out and steadied her. "Hey, you okay?"

She saw Matt, his eyes wide with concern, and then looked past him, beyond the curve of the road. What she saw both frightened and fascinated her, but reconciling those feelings amidst the bedlam in her head proved impossible. Waves of pain crashed against the inside of her skull, like the layers of her brain were being burned away.

"Katie," Matt said. "What's wrong?"

The cacophonous buzzing and chatter in Katie's head dissipated, slowly, but words continued to fail her. Instead, she pointed.

Ahead, on Samantha Walker's front lawn, stood a small cherubic figure, curiously strange but equally horrifying. It was naked and without discernable genitalia, ghost-white skin shiny, smooth, like a small mannequin. Its hands were outstretched, cradling a long red candle, a teardrop of flame flickering above it. Wax glistened and dripped like blood between the child-thing's fingers, the contrast striking even in the dark.

The thing stared at them, eyes unblinking, black and emotionless, almost alien.

Something screamed through the quiet but still present static in Katie's head—*run run RUN!* it seemed to say—but her legs refused to budge.

When Matt turned and saw the thing staring at them, he flinched and leaned back as if preparing to bolt. "What the crap is that?"

Katie cleared her throat, found her voice again. "I don't know. What do *you* think it is?"

"No idea." Matt craned his neck forward and scrunched up his face, as though he were trying to read a road sign far off in the distance. "Was it there before?"

"I don't think so," Katie said. She glanced down the street, and gasped. "Oh my God, Matt, look! They're everywhere."

There were nine houses on Farmington Circle, all clustered near its circular end. Katie had always felt close to her father here. He'd helped build every house on the street, and they stood a testament to the man he had been—quiet, strong, sheltering. She felt protected in their presence.

Now, standing before each of those homes was a perfectly still child clutching a dark red candle, and Katie no longer felt safe.

"I don't get it." Matt shook his head.

She didn't get it either, but she felt a jagged blade of fear scraping its way down her spine. She loved horror—books, movies, music—but the image before her was too spooky, too real.

A darkness comes, child, a single voice said, entering her mind uninvited, as smooth and cold as an icicle.

"What?" she said.

"I said—"

"No. Not you."

Matt cocked an eyebrow, made a fist, and spoke into it: "Crazy Katie Bananas, this is Big Daddy Matt, come again? Over. *Ksssh.*"

The blade of fear grew still at the small of her back, its tip piercing her skin with slow, steady persistence.

"Did you hear anything?" she asked, unable to look away from the child.

Matt's brow crinkled like a pile of discarded wrapping paper on Christmas morning. "You okay?"

"Never mind," she said, massaging her temples. "I don't like this."

"Word up on that, sista. This is either a stupid joke, or everyone on this street is in a weirdo cult. Maybe both. Sure you're okay?"

She nodded. But Katie couldn't shake the feeling that something beyond their understanding, something unnatural—even supernatural—was happening. A big pill to swallow, but the alternative—that she was bat-shit crazy—was much bigger, and she wasn't quite ready to gulp that one down.

"Can we go?"

"Yeah, sure."

Matt picked up his candy, and together they walked into the unknown.

* * *

Matt crossed the front lawn of his home, his movements bold and purposeful. His footsteps darkened the dew-covered grass with each step. As he drew closer to the figure he slowed, hesitated, and then stopped a few feet away.

You must run, flee. A darkness comes.

"Matthew," Katie said, tugging on his arm like a toddler trying to get her mother's attention. "Can we *please* go inside?"

She looked back over her shoulder, half expecting to see an army of porcelain-skinned children creeping up on them, claws and fangs bared. But still they stood, one on each front lawn, blank-faced and unmoving.

"It's fake," Matt declared. He was staring into the black orbs that served as the child's eyes. "Christ, what a bizarre prank." He chuckled like a mad professor up to no good in his la-*bor*-atory, though Katie knew it was a nervous kind of laughter.

"Matthew, it's real." She wasn't sure why she believed this, because it made no more sense than any other tale this holiday had been built upon, but she knew it was true. She *felt* it, heard it loud and clear.

"What? Come on! It's fake," he insisted. "Probably a plastic Halloween prop—a weird one—or some wacky Japanese candleholder. They never get that shit right."

"I'm hearing a voice, something...I don't know, Matt, but I don't like it. We have to go."

"Go where?" Matt said, his confusion fueled by her own. "Isn't this where we were going?"

Behind Matt and his incredulous stare, the child's mouth opened impossibly wide. A panicked squeal escaped Katie's lips. She lurched backward, stumbled over one of Mrs. Hapler's juniper shrubs that adorned the lawn, and landed hard on her backside.

Matt spun around, screamed when he saw the gaping mouth, and defensively swung his candy-laden pillowcase. It slammed into the child's chest. Candy exploded around them. The candle tumbled from the child's grasp, flame flickering to nothing as it rolled across the wet lawn.

In response, the voice in Katie's head sliced through her like a hail of razors, no words, just an agonizing howl—and she howled with it.

The child's eyes cataracted before them. Its statuesque stance faltered, and it crumpled to the ground. A few inches away, a curl of smoke rose from the crimson candle, disappeared into the night like a spirit gone home.

Katie scrambled to her feet, her pillowcase and candy forgotten among the shrubbery.

"Did you see that?" Matt said, nearly screeching the words. "Jumpin' Jesus on a pogo stick! Did you *see* that?"

"I saw," she said.

Matt turned around, and Kate watched the color drain from his face like a cartoon character seeing a ghost, as if he were becoming one of the mysterious children.

"Holy goddamn crap," he whispered.

"I'm okay," she said.

"Not you. Look."

Katie followed his gaze and the blade of fear sliced through her spine, paralyzing her.

A soft orange glow spread across James Rothney's front lawn. There, another child stood, surrounded by the delicate light of a fire—which emanated not from without but from *within* its body. Its eyes were deep pools of flickering fire, its skin the pink-orange of a midsummer sunset. The child stood at attention, hands dripping with what appeared to be blood. The candle was gone.

Up and down the street, the children stood still as soldiers, sentries burning with an inner flame, like pumpkins.

Like pumpkins...

Pumpkins...

It echoed through the halls of her mind...and then she understood.

Katie had attributed her fear to the mere presence of the children, but all at once the shades of ignorance lifted and the sunshiny rays of realization illuminated her thoughts: The children weren't there to harm them.

Like fucking pumpkins!

"My god," she said. "What have you done?"

Katie rushed past Matt, and fell to her knees beside the seemingly lifeless ghostchild. "Help me," she said. "Quickly!"

The child's hands were streaked with red as though it had been freshly crucified, its body tossed aside for scavengers to feast upon. Katie's hand closed around the child's fingers, now paler than before, and a cold river flooded her veins, stomped through her bones like Death marching. She gasped for air.

The voice came again, unbidden as before, with such urgency it threatened to unhinge her sanity.

Darkness! You must flee the darkness, child! They come!

The world around her flickered like an old television transmission. She clenched her eyes tight, and her mind filled with the image of her father, smiling, radiant. He held his finger to his lips, like he had done so many times before when he wanted her to stop talking and just listen. The scene within her mind faded to Bridgetown Pines, as if she were standing in the middle of Farmington Circle with a million compound eyes at her disposal, each one helping piece together fragments of a single scene...

The ghostly procession emerges from the woods, and one by one the strange beings split from the group to stand like watchmen around the homes of the Pines' residents...

Some turn and face the street, while others disappear behind the homes...

They hold out their palms like children collecting snowflakes...

Drops of red fall from the sky, into their upturned hands, and the red rises, rises, rises, until a single flaming teardrop descends from the heavens, burning bright...

Katie and Matt appear at the far end of the street, they linger in front of Samantha's house, and then they're standing before the child on Matt's front lawn...

And then...

And then...

And then the darkness moves...

Thick strips of black break away from the shadows, undulating through the air like heartworms heading for the heart of the world. Bloodcurdling whispers echo down the street as if all the damned souls of Hell were marching to war, singing songs of deliverance...

The mass of shadows turn as one...

Katie's eyes jerked open. For a moment she thought she was emerging from a nightmare, safe and sound under a tangle of blankets while the warm sun peeked through the blinds of her bedroom window.

But there was no sun, no warmth, just an icy realization that, if anything, the nightmare had just begun.

* * *

"What the hell, Katie?" Matt knelt beside her, a look of profound fear and confusion contorting his face.

The sweet smells of myriad candies floated up Katie's nostrils and down her throat, and she had to swallow to keep from throwing up. "What happened?"

"You tell me," he said. "First you're scolding me like I'm two, and then you're grabbing onto this stupid thing, twitching and muttering like a lunatic. What the hell?"

"How long was I like that?"

"I don't know. Ten, maybe twenty seconds."

Katie tried to resolve that in her muddled head. How had she seen so much in such a short period of time? She looked down at the child and the vision returned, this time from her own memory. She saw the black things detach from the shadows, twisting through the trees. She saw her father...

Her mind reeled.

She looked toward Samantha's place. Samantha, who had recently lost her daughter—her only child—at the hands of an unlicensed drunk driver. And James Rothney's father had just passed, at the age of 101, outliving all his siblings by two decades. Katie's mind moved from house to house. Carmen Langford...husband...lung cancer. Dead. Garret Wilson...son...overdose. Dead. Melinda and Ray Kingsbury, Ian Millhouse, Sarah Forest, Tamara Jenkins...each of them had recently lost family members.

"Unlock the door," she said. "We need to get inside."

"Are you listening to yourself? Jesus Christ! You're going crazy right before my frickin' eyes."

"Now!"

Spurred on by her commanding tone, Matt thrust his hand in his pocket, pulled out his keys, and stepped past her, his face twisted into an aggravated sneer. He made to kick the prone child on his lawn, but seemed to think better of it, and headed toward the house.

Katie turned and watched the child holding vigil on Samantha's lawn down the street. The fire burned strong from within, but then, ever so slightly, it dimmed as if battling a biting wind. The flame shivered and pulsed and faltered to an ember.

Then, slowly, like the awakening of dawn, the small glow within the child brightened, brightened, and brightened more, until it repelled the darkness once again.

As if warding off evil spirits...

As if the vision she saw through the eyes of the fallen child had come true.

Though she couldn't see anything now, she knew that the flickering of light was a battle being waged and that the darkness had been repulsed by whatever force the child commanded.

Darkness comes, she thought.

It was only a matter of time before that darkness got to Matt's house.

Katie crossed the lawn and took all three porch steps in one stride. Inside, Matt pulled out a chair at the kitchen table. He sat down heavily, grabbed a red Granny Smith apple from the centerpiece, and began rolling it back and forth between his hands.

"I need fire," Katie said.

"You need therapy," Matt said, not looking up.

"Shut up and help me, Matthew! We haven't got time."

"Time for *what*, exactly?" He stared at her, defiant. The red apple rolled to a stop before him like a heart that had ceased beating. "Are you in on this prank—trying to creep me out, scare me?"

"It's not a goddamn prank," she said, crossing the kitchen to stand before him. She softened her voice, hoping to calm his nerves. "The thing on the lawn, the child, it's here to protect us—they're here to protect everyone."

"Oh, right. Of course!" He slapped the tabletop. "It all makes sense now."

Katie ignored him. She told him of her vision, the black things, her father, everything, and when she finished she had to admit it sounded downright nutso.

"And you think it's real," he said.

She nodded, ignoring his derisive tone. Crazy-sounding or not, Katie didn't *think* anything. She *knew*. Her father had come to her from a place beyond this world, free of disease, free of pain, happy. The children were some sort of avatars or manifest protectors, sent by her father and by the recently-passed family members of Matt's neighbors. She knew it with all her heart.

As if reading her thoughts and intent on shattering them, Matt asked: "But what about the Samsons? They're *both* dead now."

Katie's confidence deflated. He was right. Mr. Samson died two days ago after a short bout with pneumonia; his funeral was being held Tuesday afternoon. Her theory had a gaping hole from which reason bled freely. Matt hadn't lost any family members, either.

Despite her faith, her desire to believe, skepticism of an afterlife—Heaven and Hell, and all that religious hoo-ha—slammed against her newfound hope.

But she was here, and her father had passed. There was that. She wanted to—*had* to—believe it was possible that her sweet, gentle father was somehow still looking out for her.

Her mind raced and her thoughts ricocheted through her head in a tangled mess of self-doubt.

Matt's smug smile hurt.

"Molly," she said, grasping for an answer. But it made sense. Sort of.

"Really. A dog?"

"Yeah, a dog. A dog that's *alive!*" Molly was still living in the Samson's home. Paula Bell, their neighbor, had been feeding and walking her since Mr. Samson was admitted to the hospital. It was a stretch, but could the Samsons be protecting their dog? Of course they could. Molly had been like a child to them.

Or maybe it wasn't so simple. *Goddamn!* If only she could put the pieces together...

"You're nuts." Matt laughed, a good old *guffaw*. "Crazy-looking midget angels descend from Heaven to protect...wait for it—" he held up a finger "—a dog."

And us, she wanted to shout. She had the urge to smack him right across his smirking face. She loved his sense of humor, his ability to turn even the most mundane circumstances into an adventure, but sometimes he just didn't listen. Usually it was over something so trivial it didn't matter.

But *this* mattered. *Now* mattered.

So she reached across the table and smacked him, the sharp *crack* echoing through the kitchen. Matt's head jerked to the side and a splotch of red spread across his cheek like a five-fingered disease. He turned back toward her, jaw muscles twitching, tears twinkling in his eyes. He blinked to keep the tears from falling.

"I'm sorry," she said. "I'm so sorry. But you have to listen to me."

"You hit me," he said in barely a whisper, as if in shock.

"I'm *really* sorry." She reached out and squeezed his hand. "But you need to listen. You saw that thing move. You saw it with your own eyes. I'm *not* crazy. I'm not! We're in danger, Matthew. From what, I don't know, but it's not good. Trust me, please."

He remained quiet for a long time, and it took all that Katie had not to prod him along. "Fine," he said, his voice like a soft breeze.

"Thank you." She pulled him to his feet. "We need a lighter, and quickly."

Moving zombielike, he pulled a barbecue lighter from the kitchen drawer and followed Katie outside. She found the candle a few feet away from the child. It smelled of old copper. A tender kind of warmth flowed into her when she held it, and she smiled.

"Lift it," she said, pointing to the body at Matt's feet.

He hesitated. "For what?"

"Stop asking questions, will you? Just do it." She was running on adrenaline and instinct.

Grabbing hold of the child, Matt inhaled sharply, groaned as if he'd been punched in the stomach. His body stiffened, twitched. The green of his eyes disappeared, his pupils stretching into sightless black orbs. Drool slithered from the corner of his mouth like a glass snake and shattered on the grass below. He lurched upright, gasping for air, flailing his arms to find his balance.

"Christ," he said. "Holy fuckersucks!"

"What happened?" Katie said.

"Wow."

Matt stared down the street, wide-eyed. Katie thought about slapping him a second time. "Matt, focus! What happened? What did you see?"

"Too much," he said, turning toward her. His eyes were still wide with fear, but finally focused. "They've seen us."

"Oh no." Hands shaking, Katie flicked the lighter. The flame sputtered. She kept at it, and it caught on the third try. She held it to the candle.

There was no wick.

She placed the flame directly to the candle's tip. Nothing happened. It wouldn't catch.

"Here," Matt said. "Try this."

Kneeling, he hoisted the child to a sitting position. The child's body hung limply, its head bowed. Grabbing its hands, Matt placed them together, palms up, as if accepting sacramental bread.

Katie stood there, staring into the sky, waiting for the blood-red raindrops to fall, like they had in her vision. But again, nothing happened.

Her heart plummeted.

"Give it the candle," Matt said. "Hurry."

She silently cursed herself. This wasn't your everyday candle. She should have known better. Instantly the child reacted when she placed the candle in its palms. Its body stiffened as if air were being blown into a balloon. With Matt's help, it stood. Eyes shifted from white to black.

Matt let go and stepped back.

Flee...now...

The voice was weaker, but the urgency still clear.

Matt grabbed Kate's arm. "Let's go!"

They ran the short distance to the house. Once inside, Matt slammed the door shut, locked it, and turned out the lights. Through the window they watched a single drop of fire descend from the sky like a dying firefly.

As if praying, the ghostly sentinel bowed its head.

The air around them seemed to gasp. A fiery glow pulsed within the child, growing brighter, stronger, hungrier, the air shimmering and blurring like waves of heat over a desert highway until all was bathed in a dazzling orange hue.

Matt went to the kitchen sink and splashed water on his face. "Holy crap," he said. "Katie, come check this out."

He had moved the curtain aside and was looking out the window that faced the back yard. There, too, stood one of the strange children, surrounded by the beautiful orange sheen. Two more stood silently on the other sides of the house, four in total, all afire from within, a protective dome encapsulating the house.

They moved to the front window again and watched the street beyond. Though they couldn't see the wormlike shadows, nor truly fathom the danger, they knew where they were by the way the firelight dimmed as the dark things repeatedly tried to break through the near invisible walls that kept them at bay.

Matt pulled Katie close and kissed her forehead. "I'm sorry," he said.

She embraced him, not sure what to say. The kiss, innocent as it might have been, had sent her heart aflutter. "It's okay," she said quietly.

"So now what do we do?"

"I don't know." Katie hadn't had time to process what had already happened, let alone figure out what they should do next. Halloween had come alive in ways more real than she could ever have imagined, shattering the fictional barrier that usually separated her world from that of the dark. "We wait, I guess."

She rested her head on Matt's shoulder.

He hugged her a little tighter.

The minutes ticked by and they watched their little corner of the world through the unbelievable orange sphere.

Again Katie thought of her father. She'd felt lost since his death, but had tried to remain strong. Her mother had dealt with the loss in a completely different way—isolation, denial, anger—and Katie's relationship with her had suffered greatly.

But maybe her father was still here with them. Perhaps, with Katie's help, her mother would soon emerge from the darkness in which she had descended.

Perhaps.

Katie had always wanted to trust in what the religious folk preached, but it had always seemed so hokey. Now, however, it seemed wonderful. The possibilities warmed her heart. And even if it weren't entirely true, could believing in some higher power, having faith in it, be so terrible?

Beyond the window, past the strange child and the enchanting sphere, there lurked a darkness more menacing than Katie could ever have imagined.

She closed her eyes, thought of her father, found hope for her mother, and dared to believe.

K. Allen Wood's *fiction has appeared in* 52 Stitches, Vol. 2, The Zombie Feed, Vol. 1, *and* Epitaphs: The Journal of New England Horror Writers. *He is also the editor/publisher of* Shock Totem, *a bi-annual horror fiction magazine. He lives and plots in Massachusetts.*

For more info, visit his website at www.kallenwood.com.

THE CANDLE EATERS

BLACK MARY

by Mercedes M. Yardley

The other girl, she has eyes like oil. They're dark and black and slick. They widen like holes and one day they'll swallow me completely.

I tell her this. She smiles, just a little.

"Maybe."

I go outside to drag some heavy wood to the house. I wear a large pair of men's boots that I tie as tightly as I can, but I still step out of them. I'm not allowed to have a pair that fits.

The wood is running low and this worries me. I remember the first nights here, the howling of the wolves in the freezing darkness, venturing from the forest that looms on the edge of the fields. The dank little house doesn't have windows that fully shut. There's no way to keep the wind out.

"If you bring me an axe, I'll chop my own wood," I had told him. I stood there in bare feet, hugging my arms around my torn dress. "You won't have to do anything. I'll do all the work for you."

He hit me then, once, hard enough that it knocked me to the ground and I couldn't get up right away. Black Mary crouched over me like a cat, hissing at him. He didn't seem to notice her.

Later he took me to his bed, gently rubbing my freezing arms and legs. The black-haired girl stood in the doorway, silently. I met her eyes over his greasy shoulder.

"Little girls aren't meant to use axes, honey," he said. "What if you hurt yourself? Nobody is here to help you, not for miles. It isn't safe. Do you understand?"

I wanted to tell him that I would be careful, that I was almost eleven years old, but I only nodded, my hands clasped between my knees.

"Tell ya what I'll do. I'll bring in wood when I come, okay? Lots of it. Will that make you happy?"

I nodded, and the gentle caress on my arm turned into something different. The girl turned away and I squeezed my eyes shut.

That was two days ago. Now the black-eyed girl stands behind me, brushing my hair. "He wears a wedding ring," she says. "That

109

means he has a wife. Maybe some kids. Maybe his kids are the same age you are."

I turn my head to the side and throw up. "Sorry," I say, and wipe my mouth with the back of my hand.

She steps in front of me and crouches until we're eye level. "Don't you ever apologize to me, get it? I'm your friend. I love you, real love, nothing like what *he* says love is." Her eyes burn, scorch, like watching fire rush across oil. "I'd like to kill him."

"You wouldn't!"

Black Mary was fierce. "I would. He knows it. Why doesn't he leave an axe here, huh? Because he knows I'd kill him one day. I'd take it and swipe at his head when he wasn't looking. Or even when he *is*. Either way."

I back up a little. She snorts.

"What, I'm too harsh for you? Are you scared, sweet little thing?" She stands up, tossing her hair back. "This is why he takes you, you know. You and not me. Because you give in. Because you're so good and quiet, and men love little girls who are quiet. Me?" She shrugs. "Nobody loves me. Not anymore."

She turns and walks away. It hurts me to see her go, but I have other things to tend to. I still have bruises inside and out. I still have the nightmares.

Black Mary is gone for several days. I look for her on the horizon, but there isn't anything besides fields of weeds. The food is almost gone. I'm hungry and sick and almost want the man to come again so that I can have something to eat. Almost.

"That's what he wants, you know," Black Mary says to me. She's sitting on a large rock out in the field. Her pointed nose and shiny hair remind me of a raven. A crow. Something that could simply fly away.

"Why did you come back?" I ask her.

"Didn't you miss me?" She tilts her head, again like a bird. I wonder if she sheds her skin at night and there are feathers underneath.

"Of course I missed you. I missed you so much. But weren't you free? Didn't you get away? Why would you come back?"

She reaches for my hand but I pull it away.

"Do you remember your mother?"

I freeze. "Why?"

BLACK MARY

My mother wore yellow dresses and grew lavender in the front yard. Her eyes were brown, like mine. Or maybe they were blue.

"Do you think she's out there looking for you?"

I sit down, my back against the rock. My stomach is hurting.

She isn't letting it go. "Do you?"

I want to think so. But it's been so long. She's probably given up by now. I wipe my face with my sleeve.

"Know what I think?"

I shake my head.

She slides off the rock and grabs my wrists. She's careful of the bruises. She always has been. "I think moms never stop looking for their kids. Not ever. No matter how long it has been."

"I don't look the same anymore."

"No, you don't. You've grown a lot in the last few years."

"What if she doesn't recognize me?"

"I think she would."

I cough and the black-eyed girl pulls away. "Come on. We need to get you inside. You're getting sick and you remember what that's like. Maybe when he comes back, he'll bring more wood."

He doesn't. He doesn't bring much food, either, just a cheeseburger from a fast food place and a shopping bag full of apples.

"Is...is there anything else?" I ask, and I pay for it. The girl with the black hair helps me up and stands behind me while I wash the blood from my dress. I meet her eyes in the mirror.

"Something's wrong, did you notice?" Her arms are folded across her chest. "See how he's pacing like that? Be careful."

He barks for me and I come. The girl was right. Something is wrong.

"Have you been out of this house, Mary?" he demanded.

My name isn't Mary. I told him that once, but he didn't care. We're all Mary here.

"Yes, sir. Just to the field and the wood pile."

"No farther?"

"No, sir." There isn't anywhere else to go. Nothing but fields and rocks and animals that run through the grass.

He leans close, his face red and his eyes wild. I flinch and this seems to make him angrier.

"You afraid of me, girl?"

I don't know what to say. His fist rises. The girl with the black hair stands behind him, her eyes huge. They're leaking oil. I'm still staring at her when he hits me the first time. A few more blows and I squeal, "How come you only hurt me and not Black Mary?" The second I say it I wish I could take it back. "I'm sorry, I'm sorry," I tell her, but she crouches in the corner, her hands over her ears, facing away from me.

The man demands to know if I love him. I try to say no. I try to say yes. My mouth is too swollen to work properly. The man stares at me in a new way and leaves. He's never left before morning before. Even though I'm grateful, my stomach twists and I'm afraid.

A new girl arrives with the sunrise. She's younger than I am. She has curly red hair and freckles. Like me, she's in a torn dress. Like me, her feet are bare.

"Who are you?" I ask. It hurts to move my jaw.

"This is Red Mary."

The girl with the black hair has bruises around her eyes. Her long hair has been cut, shaggy and boyish, like mine. She has displeased him.

"What happened to you?" I want to ask, but I'm afraid that she'll tell me. He found her. He went to her. I pointed her out and she isn't safe anymore.

Red Mary speaks. Her voice is tremulous, soft like tiny bells. "He asked me if I liked toys. He said that we could play games."

I turn and look at her. Seize her arm, yank up her sleeve. Her skin is white, without marks in the shape of his fingers. Her eyes are scared but not horrified. Not yet.

"He said that to me," I told her. I grab her hand. She grabs back.

"He said that to me, too." Black Mary's voice has changed. It sounds tired, more like mine. Like she's given up.

I'm not giving up. Not if we can save Red Mary.

"We need to go," I say. The girls look at me. I swallow hard. "We need to go."

"Go?" Red Mary asks. She's so trusting. She's holding onto a grey stuffed bunny that I hadn't noticed before. I had one just like it when I was little.

"He'll hurt you," I tell her. "He'll keep you here and do...horrible things."

She starts to tremble. "What kind of things?"

My breath hitches and I can't talk for a minute. I catch Black Mary's eye. One is starting to swell shut, but she still tries to smile at me.

"If he catches you, he'll kill you," she says. "You know that he will."

I know.

I don't have anything to take with me except the apples. I shove my feet into the too-big shoes and stuff them with newspaper. It had snowed during the night. I wish that I had a coat.

"Now we run," I say, and take Red Mary by the hand. My muscles ache and new cuts from last night open up. But we keep moving.

"I'm tired," Red Mary says after a few hours. "I want to go back."

I shake my head. "You don't."

Black Mary climbs beside me. She isn't even breathing heavy.

"Do you remember," she says, "when we tried to run away before? You were little, just like Red Mary. We got about this far and then you turned back."

I'm shocked. "Did I? Why would I do that?"

She shrugs. "You didn't know any better. You didn't know what he was like then."

My sides hurt. My feet are blistered, but I know that if I stop he'll catch me. There was something wrong last night, something in his eyes that makes my mouth go dry.

"He's in trouble. Maybe somebody knows. Or maybe," Black Mary says, blood running from the corner of her mouth, "you're too old."

"What do you mean, too old?"

"You know what I mean."

The snow starts to fall again. The cough from earlier deepens in my lungs.

"Are you going to die?" Red Mary asks. She's skipping through the snow, not seeming to feel the cold.

"That's not a nice thing to ask," Black Mary scolds. Her hair is back to its long, shiny length, her black eyes healed.

"But is she? Are you?" Red Mary turns to me. I don't know what to say.

Black Mary lies down in the snow. "Maybe I'll just wait here until he finds me. Oh, he's going to be so *mad.*" Her eyes glitter. "Don't you think he'll be *mad?*"

"You need to stand up," I tell her, and pull at her arm. Suddenly I realize that she is the one who is standing. I'm lying in a snowdrift, my hair blowing over my face. I had almost fallen asleep.

"Run," she says, and Red Mary echoes her. "Run."

It's getting dark now. I scramble to my knees and crawl through the snow, not strong enough to run. At least the burning pain of freezing to death makes me think of something other than my bruises.

There's a light. It's small and beautiful. I ask the girls if they see it.

"What light?" Black Mary asks, and she falls.

"I'm cold," Red Mary whispers, and she also falls.

I try to drag Red Mary but I only get a few feet. She's too heavy. I'm too cold.

"I'll get help," I say, but they don't answer.

The light is coming from a window in a small house on the edge of a field. It looks like it might be painted yellow. I think my mom's house was yellow.

"It was, when you were younger," Black Mary says. She's crawling through the snow with me.

"Feeling better?" I ask her.

Her eyes are like ice. "No."

We make it to the porch. I'm on my knees, hesitating. Black Mary puts her hand on my shoulder.

"We can always go back if you want."

I knock on the door. The bones in my hands feel like they'll shatter from the cold.

A shadow moves in the window. I want to scream, and I do. Shadows hit and twist and bite. Shadows hurt you from the inside out.

The shadow opens the door. It is a woman. She looks at me and her hand goes to her mouth.

"Oh my goodness. Oh no," she says. She calls over her shoulder for a blanket and some hot chocolate and the police. She looks back at me, reaching out with both hands. She touches my skin and we both draw back.

"Are you alone, sweetheart?"

BLACK MARY

Black Mary sweeps past her into the house. Red Mary sits on the porch, sucking her thumb.

"You're too old to do that," I tell her. I look back at the woman.

"My mom had a yellow house, I think. Do you know my mom?"

The blanket arrives. She spreads it out and I gingerly step into it, my eyes on Black Mary. She nods, and I let the woman wrap it around me and lead me inside.

"What's your name, sweetie?" The woman is all eyes, taking in my tattered dress and ratted hair, the bruises and dried blood. I want to say that she should check on Red Mary, but the little girl seems happy. She seems okay.

My name. It's been too long. I scribbled it on the page of a book once, but he threw all of the books away one day when he was angry.

"I can't remember. I'm just one of the Marys."

The woman's voice is patient, carefully so. "One of the Marys? Which one?"

A man enters the room, saying something about the police being on their way. I see him and shrink back. He is big and tall and his hands could wrap around my throat so easily. The man looks like he wants to say something, but he only uses his big hands to pass a mug to the woman and then steps away.

"Which Mary?" the woman asks again. Her eyes are soft. She shows me that the mug is full of hot cocoa.

"I don't know. Maybe White Mary. Do you think my mom will remember me?"

Red Mary taps the woman on her thigh. "We're all Mary here," she tells her, but the woman doesn't look at her. Not once. She doesn't even seem to notice.

Mercedes M. Yardley *wears red lipstick and poisonous flowers in her hair. She has been published in John Skipp's* Werewolves and Demons *anthologies,* The Pedestal Magazine, The Vestal Review, *and* A Cup of Comfort for Parents of Children with Special Needs. *Mercedes is the Nonfiction Editor for* Shock Totem: Curious Tales of the Macabre and Twisted.

EXHIBIT C

By David McAfee

A h, good. Right on time, sweetheart. I'm gettin' pretty good at measurin' doses; I had your timin' down perfect. Of course, it helped that I knew your weight, even if you tried to keep that shit secret. But I knew it. I always knew it, even when you'd lie and say a different number. I knew you were lyin', I just didn't care. I...

Oh, shit. Hold on. Let me get the tape recorder goin'...

There. Now we can start. So, didja miss me?

Damn! If you arch your back any harder you're gonna break your spine, hon. Sorry, I shoulda told you about my little friend, there. His name is Merle, after Merle Haggard. He's just a plain ol' rat. Like him?

Right, right. Of course you don't. You were always scared of rats. Pretty silly, if you ask me. The things are mostly harmless. That's why I stuck Merle in there with you, so you could see he's just a cute little furball. You guys are gonna get along fine.

Don't bother strugglin'. Those cuffs held that cop for half a day before I finally did him a favor and broke his shins. They'll hold you just fine. But, since I remembered how much you like kinky shit, I had 'em padded just for you. Whaddya think? Just like old times, right? Ha! Okay, maybe not so much. Still, you're cuffed, and I'm standing next to you. That's gotta bring back a few memories, don't it? I know this ain't the same as bein' cuffed to the bed, but it'll do. The bed is still upstairs, but I needed somethin' different for the basement. Somethin' stronger. Somethin' that wouldn't absorb the blood like a mattress.

That's why you're layin' in a big marble box. Took me a while to make it, especially since I had to scrounge the marble from foreclosed houses and the like. I couldn't just walk into Home Depot and ask for pieces to make a marble box three feet deep and six feet long. That woulda looked kinda funny, don't you think? Woulda given the cops too much info, too. Took fuckin' forever to cut the slabs and secure 'em together, too. You wouldn't believe how heavy that shit is. But it had to be marble. I know how much

117

you like marble, plus blood just washes right off that shit. A little water, a little bleach, and presto! Clean as a freshly-wiped baby's ass.

Oh, looks like Merle found your toe. Come on, now. It's just a little nibble. No need for such a fuss.

You know, hon, you really should see your face right now. I'm tempted to take a picture so you can check out your expression, but that's probably not a good idea. I dunno much about that shit, and I'd probably send the fuckin' pic somewhere by accident, and that'd be the end of me. We don't want that, do we? Of course not.

Anyhoo, I bet you're surprised to see me again, ain'tcha? After all, it's been six years since you met Brian and took off. What have you been up to? Oh, right. The gag. Sorry. I'm working on a new place that will let me stop using those things, but for now I can't have you screamin'. The neighbors might hear. So far this setup has worked pretty good, at least it suited for the last few people. It should work just fine for you, too.

Don't matter anyway. I know what you've been up to. It took me a long time to find you again, but once I tracked you down it was easy enough to see what you've been doin' the last six years. For example, you taught my son that Brian is his father, and then you went and gave him a little brother. Still sittin' on your ass at home, too. No job for you. Poor Brian. How many hours a week is that sap workin' to keep you happy? 60? 70? What a dipshit. I might have to pay him a visit next. Nah, that's probably a bad idea. It's bad enough I grabbed you, but if he disappeared too, it'd point the cops right at me. They're already lookin' harder since I put that detective up on that cross. Did you see the news reports? I especially loved the shot from that one photographer; the one that showed the big metal cross stickin' up outta the dirt with the detective's body hangin' from it. That shit was cool. It was a bitch gettin' that damn cross out of the basement and planting it in the park like that, but it was worth it. They showed that picture on every TV news show from California to New York. I'm famous now.

And you always said I was a bum who'd never make anything of myself. Guess I showed you.

Merle sure seems to like your toe. No matter how many times you kick him away, he just keeps comin' back. My fault. I forgot to feed him the last couple of days. Sorry, Merle.

It's their own fault, really. That detective was a joke. Them givin' my case to him was a slap in the face. Told me they didn't

EXHIBIT C

take me serious. Made me realize I had to do somethin' big to get their attention. It worked. But now that I got it, I gotta be extra careful. That's why I have the saw, but we'll get to that in a minute. First we're gonna have a little fun.

Ha! You should see your eyes! I swear they are the size of apples! Relax, hon. Not *that* kind of fun. If I wanted to fuck you I'd have already done it. You ain't exactly in a position to resist, y'know. I won't lie, I thought about it. After all, you fucked me pretty hard when you left. Divorce papers served in absentia. The fuck was that about? Still, I'm over it.

No, really. I am. That shit's got nothin' to do with why you're here, although I can't say I'm not glad it's you strapped to that piece of rock. Kinda like a bonus. No, see, the thing is, the cops are looking extra hard for me. I thought if I took someone from another state it might confuse 'em. And it just so happened that the P.I. I hired to find you got back to me just as I started lookin'. It felt right, y'know. It just clicked. This was perfect. No online trail to track because I didn't have to use the 'net to find my next person— amazin' how those forensic computer guys can find just about anythin', ain't it?—and now that the P.I. is toast, no human trail, either. No trace of who or what I been doin'. Even Merle, there, is a wild-caught rat. No pet stores are gonna know my face when the cops come lookin'.

Oh, I know what you're thinkin'. You're thinkin' I'm linked to the P.I., ain't you? Well, I paid the guy in cash, so there's no record, and I hired him for his reputation for discretion, so I doubt he made any notes. But I went through his office, just to be safe. The cool thing about that is I managed to get a shitload of dirt on a lot of people. That's going to make things even more fun when they catch me. Do you know what the governor of this state has been doing on our tax dollars? Shocking shit.

Oh, crap. I went off track, didn't I? That still hasn't changed. You used to say I had adult ADD, remember? I guess you mighta been right. I can never stay focused on one thing for very long. That's why I brought all these toys. See? I got at least two dozen of 'em, and they are all a blast. I use one for a minute, then switch to a new one when I get bored. It's a perfect system, really. Plenty of new things to try. I ain't gotten bored yet.

Tears? Why you cryin', sweetheart? I ain't gonna use any of 'em on you. No, really. I promise. None of these shiny, bladed doohickeys are for you. Not one.

Ha! Merle must think he's your man, now. The way he's nibblin' on your ear is almost tender. He sure is friendly, isn't he? That's gotta sting a bit, though. Y'know, I read somewhere that everywhere a male rat walks, he leaves a trail of urine 'cause his dong drags along the ground all the time. I wonder if that's true. I hope not, or you have about a dozen trails all over your body. That's kinda disgustin'. But at least you won't have to put up with it for too long.

The only real bitch about this is I can't send this tape to the cops like I did with the last two. I've said you're my ex wife on here a few times already, and I even said Brian's name. That would make it too easy for those bastards. But that's okay. I'll take this tape out and put another in just before we start. This part of the conversation is always more for me, anyway. The part I want the cops to hear is what comes next.

So, you ready?

More tears? Shakin' your head? Come on now, hon. This is no time for that. We got work to do. What are you lookin' at, anyway?

Oh, right. The saws. Don't worry. Those are for later. I gotta take a few steps to hide your identity from the police. Gonna be hard for 'em to figure out who you are without fingerprints and shit. By the way, you still got that tattoo on your ass? Never mind, I'll find out myself after it's over. As a bonus, Brian and the boys won't know what happened to you. You'll have just disappeared one day and never come back. I like that idea. That's what happened, after all. You left this house one day and just never came back.

But like I said, I'm over it. Mostly.

It's time to get started. Let me change over the tape real fast.

Okay. Done.

This is the tape I'm gonna give the cops.

Hi cops! Ha ha ha. It's me again.

That reminds me of that Ray Stevens song, "It's Me Again, Margaret." Funny shit. You ever heard it? Crap. You can't talk. I keep forgetting about the gag. Just nod or shake your head.

No? Don't wanna? Fair enough. I guess I can't blame you, what with Merle takin' chunks outta your cheek like that. Anyway, it's been nice catchin' up, but I think we need to speed this along, don't you?

EXHIBIT C

Oh, so *now* you can shake your head. You got a nice, wide stubborn streak, don'tcha?

Anyway, as you can imagine, it's gonna take Merle an awful long time to finish the job. I ain't got that kinda time. That's why I brought a few of his friends over. Check this out.

Oooof! This box is fuckin' heavy.

There. Got the top off. Here you go, honey. Here are some more friends to play with. Three dozen of 'em, to be exact. Took me forever to catch all of 'em. I made sure they were all males, too. Call me old fashioned, but havin' females in there would just feel *weird*, y'know? I guess that means you gotta put up with the urine trails. Sorry about that.

But don't worry, I'll stay here with you until it's over. And since you got that gag, you can scream as loud as you want. That should help a little.

Wow. You're gonna break your spine doin' that.

David McAfee *is the author of many books, including* 33 A.D., 61 A.D., The Dead Woman (The Dead Man #4), *and* Saying Goodbye to the Sun. *His stories have appeared in numerous anthologies, including his own collections* The Lake and 17 Other Stories *and* Devil Music and 18 Other Stories. *David lives a currently nomadic existence with his loving wife and two wonderful children. To read more about his ideas, works, and general musings, visit http://mcafeeland.wordpress.com.*

THE CANOE

by Joel Arnold

He lives with his son in a cabin next to a cold, rusty river. The rust reminds Tab of blood spilled in the Mekong. His blood. His mother and father's blood. Caught in a hail of bullets as they swam toward freedom. But that was many years ago, and this rust comes from the taconite processing plant twenty miles upstream.

His cabin has two bedrooms, a small living room, a kitchen, a bathroom, a fireplace that pops and hisses during the winter and the cool, spring nights. Tab wishes his wife were still alive. She always talked about living in a home with a fireplace.

* * *

The Kraemer River smells like fish and rust and pine. The walleyes and northerns are sparse, and those caught are thrown back in. The DNR says the mercury levels are too high, that eating the fish is dangerous. But sometimes Carl and Tab sit on the bank and throw in their lines and struggle with the slippery fish, reel them in with whoops of joy, admire them briefly, and throw them back in. It's times like those when Tab feels he's getting his son back.

* * *

Forest. Deer. Moss. Pine. The air tastes sweet and cool. The sun is a mellow orb through the trees, the rays neither harsh nor demanding. The forest can be dark, even when the sun is high in the clear sky, but the pine and birch branches shelter, they do not menace. A big change from New York City. No gangs. Carl is sixteen now.

"Are you bored here?" Tab asks.

"Sometimes."

"What about your school friends?"

Carl shrugs.

Life is so much better here. During the year, Carl became involved in basketball, his grades improved. Good people here.

123

Carl says, "People in school call me a gook."

Tab's smile vanishes. "What? Why is this the first time I'm hearing this? Who calls you that?"

"Some of the kids."

"Which kids?"

"I don't know. It doesn't matter, anyway."

"When did they call you this?"

"A bunch of times." Carl looks at his father, his eyes steady and cold. "I didn't tell you because I didn't want us to move again."

"You know why we moved."

"I liked New York. I had friends there."

"Thugs and hooligans. We live here now. These are good people. Maybe some are ignorant, but soon they'll see we're good people, too." Tab smiles encouragingly at his son. "We'll survive here. We will, Carl. We'll survive."

* * *

An aluminum canoe with fading red paint washes up on shore while Tab and Carl cast their lines to the river's poisonous fish. There is crude lettering on the bow. FARBANTI. There are dents, too, but they can be pounded out with a rubber mallet.

"Help me push this out into the river," Tab says.

"Why don't we keep it?"

"Because. Maybe someone is waiting for it."

They slide it over the muddy bank into the water where the current takes hold. It straightens like the needle of a compass and disappears into the evening's dim light.

* * *

New York. As many people as insects. Ceaseless noise.

But this is where Tab married. Where Carl was born. Where Mina died.

One sweltering night, when Carl was only fourteen, there was a knock on the apartment door. Rare to get visitors. Tab opened the door a crack, leaving the chain attached.

Carl. In handcuffs. Smelling of beer. Cigarettes. A cut on his face. An ugly bruise. Suspended between two policemen.

"This your kid?"

THE CANOE

Tab unlatched the chain and opened the door wide. "Yes, this is my son."

"We saw him jump out of a van, throw a punch at a college student. When we intervened, the van took off."

"Is this true?" Tab asked.

Carl's jaw was set. He stared at the floor, breathing sharply through his nose.

"He said it was his initiation into the Laughing Tigers. A Vietnamese gang."

"We're Cambodian. American, now."

"Yeah, well. He didn't give us much trouble, said he lived here. I told him as long as you were home, we'd turn him over to you." The cop unfastened the handcuffs. Carl hurried past Tab into the apartment. "Keep an eye on him," the cop said. "I won't be so nice next time."

"Yes, sir," Tab said. "Thank you."

* * *

How do you keep hold of your son, your only son, the only family you have left, when you don't know what he does during the day? When he doesn't come home until two in the morning on school nights?

You move. Move someplace safe.

* * *

The river. Always moving. Giving and taking with indifference.

The canoe washes up again, its stern caught on the protruding roots of an ash tree. The bow bobs in the flowing river.

Farbanti.

Again, Carl asks, "Can we keep it?"

Tab looks up and down the river, wondering where it came from. "If no one else claims it." He pulls it onto the shore so the tug of current won't reclaim it. "Go inside and grab some rope. We'll tie it to this tree for now."

"Let me take it out on the river," Carl says. A warped paddle lies across the canoe floor. Carl looks up at his father. "Come with me. It'll be fun."

"Neither of us knows how to ride this."

"I do. It's easy."

"I don't think—"

Carl shoves the canoe into the water and straddles the bow. "Forget it," he says. "I'll go myself." He pushes off from shore, carefully steps across the bottom to the stern, sits, picks up the paddle, and straightens the canoe.

"Be careful," Tab calls.

Carl and the canoe slip easily around a bend in the river and disappear from view.

* * *

Tab fashions a flier on yellow paper and carries it to the roadhouse. There is no community center up here, no coffee shop, no VFW. There is only the roadhouse, and if anything needs to be said or learned, this is the place to go.

Tab sits at the bar. "Anybody missing a canoe?" he asks Jim, the bartender.

"Haven't heard anything." Jim pours a cup of coffee for Tab and slides a container of half-and-half across the bar.

"It washed up at our home the other day." He shows Jim the flier. "May I put this up?" He staples it to a bulletin board by the door on which other fliers announce items for sale, property for rent, dogs and cats lost and found, rides offered out of town to Duluth and the Twin Cities.

Tab comes back to his cup of coffee. Sips it. Carl has already taken the canoe out on the river each of the last two days, and was gone for hours both times. This is good for a boy his age, isn't it? Out in the forest, in the branch-filtered sun? Good exercise. Fresh air. Better than sitting in his room all day playing video games and watching television. Why is it, then, that Tab feels the familiar pangs of worry in his heart?

"Something wrong?" Jim asks.

"No." Tab looks up. "Nothing is wrong."

* * *

But what about drugs? Maybe that would explain Carl's melancholy. Once, Tab found marijuana in his room in New York. But here? Up here where there is clean air and warm sun and a pleasant river flowing nearby?

No. Not here, Tab decides. Carl's lonely. He's a young man. He has no girlfriend. That's all it is.

Three round, pink scars throb like fluttering moths on Tab's back and shoulder. Three round, pink scars left by bullets all those years ago while crossing the Mekong River. Maybe someday Tab will tell Carl about them. Maybe someday. But it is too hard to talk about now. Too hard to think about. Maybe someday.

* * *

River. Slow and steady. Carl gone all day long. What is downriver that interests a teenage boy so much? When he comes home each evening, he is full of sweat and quiet. Goes straight to his room as if he's got a secret. Three weeks have passed since the canoe showed up. Every day Carl has taken it out, letting the current ferry him away, only to come back in the evening, paddling hard.

And last night Carl didn't come back until past midnight. Tab drove the Volkswagen down a service road adjacent to the river, shining a flashlight through the trees, looking for the talcum red glow of hull in the cone of light, but saw nothing. He stopped at the roadhouse and asked if anyone had seen him. No one had. When Tab drove back to the cabin, there was Carl in bed, snoring heavily. He would wait until morning to scold him.

But come morning, Carl is gone, the rope that kept the canoe tied to the ash tree frayed and loose, floating in the river like a dead, sun-dried snake.

* * *

Tab works a drill in Walt Emory's machine shop three miles upriver. He's worked there since arriving just shy of a year ago, drilling holes in chunks of die-cast metal. But as often as he works, his mind is back there, back on the Mekong, drifting along the current. The sweat on his brow becomes river water splashed up onto him from the force of bullets.

The memories make Tab close his eyes. He tries to force the memories back so they can't overwhelm him, but sometimes they are impossible to ignore.

So long ago.

Bullets. Muddy water. Pain.

In the Mekong, thrown off the raft they had paid river pirates so much to take them on.

Mother screaming. A bullet ripping through her chest, her neck, spraying blood on the boy she carries. Tab grabs the boy, his baby brother, as his mother sinks beneath the murky water. His father is gone too, the only trace of him a brief patch of rust on the river's surface. The brother squirms in Tab's arms, screaming, crying. Bullets slap the water around them. Tab holds his breath. Holds his brother close against his chest. A bullet catches Tab in the back of the shoulder. Another in the back. Another below that. Intense pain, like spears of ice. More bullets zip past his ear, kiss the water like hot drops of rain. He smells cooked flesh—his own—where the bullets entered. Water bites into his eyes.

His brother's forehead is warm against his chin, his brother's breath is wet against his neck.

I'm sorry, brother. I'm sorry.

Tab sinks below the surface. Holds his brother with one hand, swims with the other as his brother struggles, tries to break free of Tab's weakening grip.

Underwater, the bullets sound like grease splattering on a flame. Tab swims deeper. Swims back, to the right, forward, to the right. Impossible to see past the blood rising off his wounds in the dark water. He surfaces. Takes a breath. Plunges back in.

His brother stops squirming.

I am so sorry.

*   *   *

How many times has Tab woken at night, crying, panicking, the memory so fresh and urgent? How many times has he gotten out of bed to check on Carl, to make sure he was okay, make sure he was breathing? How many times?

*   *   *

Night. Dark. The sounds of flowing water and chirruping frogs. Carl snores heavily in his room. Tab rises from bed and creeps barefoot through the cabin out onto the pine needle strewn ground. He feels his way over the short path that leads to the river, finds the rope that holds the canoe, and unties it from the tree. He tosses the loose end into the canoe and pushes until the current grabs hold. Moonlight glimmers on the water, the canoe a black void traveling slowly down the middle.

Tab walks back to the cabin, feeling guilty. Relieved.

* * *

But—morning—

Carl is gone. Tab steps into the daylight, his eyes turning to the tree where the canoe was tied, and his muscles tense at the sight of the rope secure around the tree.

How can that be? He didn't release the canoe from the rope, he released the rope from the tree. And now there it is again, tight around tree. Had he only dreamed it last night? But there on the ground are the impressions of his feet in the soft pine needles.

Did the canoe come back?

And did Carl take the canoe out again?

Tab hurries back inside and goes straight to Carl's room. He digs through the drawers, rifling through the clothes and books and videotapes. What am I looking for? Drugs? No. Maybe, yes, but...

Nothing. He finds nothing. He opens Carl's closet. Pushes the clothes aside. Freezes. Scrawled on the back of the closet wall is the word Farbanti. And curled up in the corner of the closet is a heap of black cloth. Tab picks it up and shakes it out. A black, hooded robe. And beneath that lies a bundle of black candles, bound together with the same kind of rope that held (did it really hold?) the canoe in place.

* * *

Carl comes home late. He isn't sweating.

"Where have you been?"

Carl eyes him suspiciously. "What do you mean? I was on the river."

"Where does the river take you? What do you do on the river all day? Who do you go see?" Tab holds up the robe and candles. "What are these?"

"You went in my closet?"

"Answer me!"

"Nothing. Just stuff."

"What kind of stuff?"

Carl's eyes harden. "You wouldn't understand."

And Carl's neck. A red scratch disappears beneath his shirt...

"Take off your shirt," Tab says.

"Father—"

"Now!"

Carl takes off his shirt. Tab gasps. His chest is covered with long, deep gouges.

"They're just scratches." Carl puts his shirt back on. "It's nothing."

"Who's doing this to you?"

"Friends."

"What friends? Who?"

"I'm going to my room. I want to be alone."

"No," Tab says. "What kind of friends do this? What would your mother say?"

"I don't care what Mom would say. She's not—"

Tab grabs Carl tightly by the throat.

Carl's eyes widen. "Stop it. You're choking me."

Tab shakes. "Don't ever talk about your mother like that again." His anger is intense but brief. He drops his arm. Swallows. "I'm sorry."

Carl sucks in his breath, chokes back tears. He turns and flees to his room, slamming the door behind him.

Soon Tab hears the sound of Carl's television, the volume shaking the small cabin's walls.

* * *

Is it gangs all over again? Even up here? In the north woods?

What can I do? Lock him in his room? Forbid him to go out? Move again?

No...

We'll survive this, Tab thinks, not really believing the words even as he thinks them. We'll survive.

* * *

The roadhouse. Packed. Loud. Full of cigarette smoke. The reek of beer.

"Who's this?" Tab scribbles Farbanti on a napkin and passes it to Jim.

Jim squints. "Hell if I know. Why?"

Tab looks up at the bartender, the only man in the area with whom he's ever had a decent conversation. His voice cracks. "I think I'm losing my son. I don't know what to do."

"He's what? Sixteen? You gotta let 'em go sometime." Jim places a shot glass in front of Tab and fills it to the rim with Jack Daniels. Tab drinks. Sets the glass down. Nods at Jim, his face blank. Jim fills it and says, "It's a bitch. Don't I know it."

* * *

Gone. When Tab gets back to the cabin that night, Carl and the canoe are gone. Tab sits at the edge of the river, throwing handfuls of sticks, pine needles, and dirt into the water. The moon is a bright pearl through the trees. A female moose splashes clumsily through the water thirty yards upstream.

Tab stands and brushes debris from his pants. When he looks downriver, he sees the black silhouette of a familiar shape. The canoe. Floating upstream against the steady current. Tab squints, shields his eyes from the glare of the moon. The canoe is empty. Tab steps back, away from the shore, as the canoe glides to a stop where he'd sat. It rocks gently from side to side as tiny ripples of water slap against its hull.

Is this a trick? Tab looks down the shore as far as he can. Is Carl just out of sight, laughing? But Tab sees no one, hears no movement.

"Carl!" he yells. He cups his hands around his mouth. "Carl!" His voice echoes through the forest, the cry of a wounded bird.

The canoe slowly turns in the water, its bow pointing downriver, yet maintains its place despite the pull of the current.

"Carl!"

Tab steps toward the canoe. He cautiously leans over it. There is only the paddle, yet its blade rests in a pool of dark liquid. Blood? It is hard to tell in only the moonlight, but if it's blood –

"Carl!" Desperate now. "Carl! Please answer!"

Nothing.

He steps warily into the canoe's stern. It wobbles, but Tab

holds out his arms and the canoe steadies. He sits carefully. Picks up the paddle. Holds it close to his face and smells the blade. Is it blood?

The canoe slips slowly from shore and the current grabs hold. Tab sits frozen in place, barely able to breath, remembering the bullets, the blood of his mother and father, remembering the moment his baby brother became still in his arms...

"No!" he cries.

He lifts the paddle. Sticks it hard in the water. If the canoe is to take him somewhere, than he'll be the one to guide it, to conform it to his own pace.

*   *   *

Sweat. Paddle. Propelling forward through the thin, rusty river.

How much loss can a man take?

He paddles on one side, then the other, determined to find his son.

Sweat. Muscles screaming.

We'll talk. About where I come from. What he means to me. We'll talk, father and son, and we'll fish and canoe together. I won't be afraid to share my pain with him. He'll understand. We'll be friends. We'll be together. We will survive.

I will not lose you.

*   *   *

A wooden flute. Voices through the trees. Tab feels eyes all around, piercing his skin. He sees torch-light in the distance.

Murmuring. Whispers. His paddling has no effect on the canoe. It slows. Drifts.

Altar. On the river. The cold, rusty river.

The canoe turns toward shore.

Chanting. The sound of the flute close by. Figures in black robes appear and pull the canoe onto gravel. The gravel scrapes the aluminum hull like bony fingers.

"Where is my son?" Tab asks, his voice unable to conceal his fear.

Pale arms appear from beneath the black robes and lift him from the canoe. He struggles, but has little strength left. They carry him to an altar made from rough planks of knotted pine and lay him on his back.

"Stop this," Tab says. "I just want my son."

They secure his wrists and ankles to the altar with copper wire. Stuff a rag in his mouth.

The chanting intensifies. Tab grows dizzy. This can't be real.

A figure leans over Tab and pulls back a deep, black hood.

Carl.

He pulls the rag out of his father's mouth.

"Carl," Tab whispers. "You don't have to do this. Please. I have so much to tell you. So much you need to know." He'll tell him of Cambodia, of the Mekong, the family who died there. He'll show Tab the bullet wounds on his back and shoulder. Then he'll understand. He'll see how much his father loves him.

"We can survive this," Tab whispers. "You and me." He smiles encouragement at his son. Nods. "We'll survive."

Carl blinks. Slowly stands. He pulls the hood back over his head, his face disappearing in shadow.

"I don't want to survive, Father." He steps back. "I want to belong." He lifts an axe high into the air. "I want to belong."

Joel Arnold's *writing has appeared in dozens of publications, with work accepted by venues ranging from* Weird Tales *and Nodin Press'* Resort to Murder *anthology, to* Amercian Road Magazine *and Cemetery Dance's* Shivers VII *anthology. Many of his short stories are available as free podcasts at Pseudopod.org, and all of his short story collections have been made available for ereaders. His horror novel* Northwoods Deep *is available in both print and electronic form. Check out his blog at* http://authorjoelarnold.blogspot.com.

DESTINATION

by Benjamin X. Wretlind

The ship swam through space, oblivious to the emptiness or the immeasurable cold that created crystalline patterns on its hull. It silently slid among the stars, between the planets, occasionally coming into contact with a stray comet or asteroid and ignoring their existence.

Inside, the atmosphere was cold, but not so immeasurable that the thermostat didn't register. Twenty-two degrees, and that was with the heating system working nonstop.

Norahc stood at the entrance to the holding bay, his fingers poised above the numbers. He lightly touched the keypad in sequence—five numbers that meant nothing, but ushered in a world of feeling.

He'd been here before...

...behind the door...

...accepting the pain unlike all the others that fought against their circumstances.

The lights above the keypad turned red. The door slid open, like a flower in spring, asking for the life-giving rain but accepting the pesky insect just the same.

The corridor in front of Norahc was lined with stasis tubes. The liquid inside glowed green, more an indication of health and wellness than an indication of operability. He methodically walked past each tube and tried his best to keep his eyes forward, away from their faces.

They were all afraid, and despite their confines and their closed eyes, he knew they waited for signs of life on the other side of the glass.

He knew what it felt like...

....behind the glass...

...accepting the loneliness and isolation that deep space offered.

Norahc stopped at the end of a row of fifty bodies, their naked, pathetic physical forms held constant in a horrific state of unrest. He'd come to ask a favor of the last—and most recent—of the travelers.

He'd come to ask for Reprieve.

The release mechanism was more secure than the door. A glowing pad registered fingerprints, a touchpad accepted his identification numbers, and a laser pointed toward his eye agreed with his last retina scan.

All of this, at least to someone so accustomed to the security, was mindless—an action performed without thought. Norahc punched in his identification, slapped his palm on the pad, and stuck his eye up to the lens. It was too routine, too comfortable, too easy to release one of the passengers.

Anyone with half a brain could do it.

Anyone with half a brain wouldn't want to do it.

The water in the stasis tube quickly withdrew with a sick sucking sound that reverberated through the holding area. The body inside collapsed into the glass in front of him. Within seconds, his eyes opened and the Panic began.

The Panic was something Norahc expected, and again he was glad the glass was thick enough to keep the body behind it at bay. The man inside screamed and pounded, kicked and screamed some more.

Norahc sat back and waited.

They had waited for him, once. When the Awakening begins and the Panic sets in, it's only natural to expect the worst but wait for the best. Father said the best never comes.

It didn't take long.

The body relaxed. The man rubbed his eyes and looked up at Norahc. His expression was less than excited, but more than nonexistent. It was, in fact, just an expression. Eyes held open, nose not flared, mouth in a state of relaxation.

No words needed to be spoken.

The man behind the glass weakly raised a finger and pointed to the door lock. Norahc held his hand over the pad one more time and waited for the green light to turn red.

Norahc was more than happy to have Reprieve. At least someone in charge was thinking clearly.

* * *

"Sleep well?" Norahc said as he studied his passenger.

"Not really, but what can you expect?"

"What's your name?"

DESTINATION

"Don't you have that on some manifest someplace?" The passenger squirmed in his seat and sipped on a cup of coffee.

"Reginald Bruce Haywood." Narohc sighed. "Yeah, I got it."

"Bruce, please. What else does it say?"

"Thirty-two years old. Cleveland native."

"Actually it's Maple Heights, but close enough."

Norahc smiled. They were always so cocky when they were released. It was almost like they expected to be treated differently just because they weren't in stasis anymore.

Arrogance was something he knew all too well, especially during Interview.

"Manifest says you killed a few people. Do you want to tell me about it?"

Bruce smiled and set his coffee cup down on the counter. The Interview room was small, but not so isolated that the outside world was nonexistent. In fact, the walls were glass, the windows nothing more than perforations.

"You know, it's cold in here." Bruce wrapped his arms around himself. "Don't you think you should turn up the heat?"

"It'll get hot enough. We're not at Destination just yet."

"And where is Destination?"

Norahc sat back in his chair and studied Bruce. His face was bruised, perhaps from the Awakening or maybe just a physical defect he brought with him. Why this ragamuffin was selected from all the others, he just couldn't say. Then again, it wasn't for him to second-guess the rules of Company. Company knows all.

"How much do you know about navigation?"

Bruce blinked. "What about my question?"

"In due time. What do you know about navigation?"

"Systems or method? I was a navigator aboard the Lincoln. I guess I can find my way around."

"How many people did you kill?"

Bruce finished what was left of his coffee and slammed it down on the table. The reaction caught Norahc off guard, and he found himself leaning forward again, his hand resting on his Stop Stick.

"You don't answer my questions, I'm not answering yours."

"Hell."

Bruce blinked. "I don't have time for metaphors. Again—you answer my question and I'll answer yours."

Norahc sat back again, relaxing his muscles. His hand dropped from the Stop Stick and reached for the carafe of coffee. He smiled inwardly at the words of his superiors, but quickly remembered their warnings as well.

"Hell," Norahc said.

Bruce sighed. His expression changed from one of anger to one so much like those before. It was resentment, futility, acceptance—all of it rolled into one.

"Fine. I killed a few people."

"Children?"

"Twenty three."

"Mothers and fathers?"

"One of each."

"Any others?"

Bruce smiled. "At least fifty. Maybe more. I lost count."

Norahc nodded. "But the State caught you."

"I guess sometimes even the best of us have to slip up."

Through the perforations, an alarm sounded, harsh but distant. Norahc stood up from his seat and walked toward a panel embedded in the wall of the room. He frowned and turned back. "Sixteen hours. We're at Proximity."

"Proximity to what?"

"Hell."

"You keep saying that. I told you I don't like metaphors."

"What would you like me to tell you?"

Bruce seemed to regard the question; his eyebrows furled and nose twitched. "You could tell me why you brought me out of stasis."

Norahc sighed. "Company selected you based on Manifest. As far as I know, you're here to relieve me."

"Relieve you? I don't know a thing about piloting a ship, just the basics of navigation."

"The ship pilots itself. From Waypoint to Destination, there's nothing you need to do except keep the controls happy and avoid any unnecessary distractions."

Bruce reached for the carafe of coffee and refilled his cup. He sat back in his chair with a smirk on his face, whatever thoughts he might have were lost inside the blackness of his eyes. For a second the relentless stare made Norahc nervous, but then again, Company had warned him.

DESTINATION

Bruce sipped from the cup and finally turned his eyes from Norahc. "What are my options?"

"Go back into stasis and accept whatever Company decides or take over for me and accept whatever Company decides. I really don't think there's an option."

"And what becomes of you?"

Norahc smiled. He wasn't sure of how to answer the question, and he felt perhaps he didn't need to. Company had provided him Reprieve and given him an out. Okay, maybe it wasn't an out, but it was a chance to relax, to stop ferrying people from Waypoint to Destination pretending he didn't care.

If only for a few days.

The smile dropped from his face as he thought of the stares, the Awakening, the Panic, and the faint glimpse of Acceptance that sparked in the eye of every passenger as they finally stepped off the ship at Destination. "Are you ready, then?"

"Ready as I'll ever be, I guess." Bruce finished his coffee and stood up. "Show me the bridge?"

"This way."

* * *

The bridge was nothing more than a small room with a window to the emptiness outside. Distant suns, faintly visible, were the only decoration on an otherwise black canvas. Below the window, a single red light blinked rapidly. Next to it there was a single red button.

"The light is the Proximity warning. You'll see that only when you're within sixteen hours. It'll blink faster the closer you get." Norahc stood at the doorway and watched Bruce take in the nothingness.

"And the button?"

"When the light stays steady, press it. That sends a signal to Gateway to open its doors."

"Sounds simple enough."

"It is simple." Norahc turned, half wishing he could tell him how much he hated the job, and half wishing he could do it himself. It wasn't the button that bothered him, nor the simplicity of the light. It was Gateway and Destination, all of it packaged together as a pill slowly eating away any bit of flesh he had left.

139

Still, the job had Meaning.

"You know, my father once told me that I'd be doomed to spend my life in service to others. It was my brother, Soré, that would get all the glory."

Bruce turned from the window. "That's a wonderful story. Anything else you want to add to that?"

Norahc frowned at the apparent sarcasm. "Yeah. I gave my father everything. Soré gave everything to others. Love and Death—they're opposites, but married to a common thread."

"I don't follow you."

"I sometimes have to look in the mirror to see what's really going on. It was my father that created Gateway, and my father that damned Destination. What I do for him is something very few people could do themselves. Soré wouldn't have any of it. If you pull yourself back for just a moment and see the grand scheme of things, then you'd see where we all fit in.

"You have a chance to be a part of that. Just remember that sometimes it's the simple things that get us through the day."

Bruce stood in silence. Norahc guessed he really didn't understand.

In time, he would.

Norahc stepped away from the door. "Just watch the light. Company will do the rest." He put his hand against the wall and the door slid shut.

"Thank you."

* * *

Norahc slept.

For the first time in ages, he closed his eyes against the world around him, blocked out everything he'd ever seen, and slept. Dreams wouldn't come, but at the very least there was relaxation. The stasis tube he placed himself in was Bruce's—the only empty place to hide. In a few hours, Company would open Gateway, Destination would accept the ship, and Awakening would begin.

For once, he didn't need to be a part of it all. They promised to leave him alone, long enough to rest, to recuperate, to regain his strength.

DESTINATION

Bruce would be fine. Despite his gruff exterior and cocky attitude, he seemed like a good pick. Norahc was pleased with Company's selection.

Evil is bound to repeat evil.

Death is a beginning.

Eternity is chaos.

* * *

The water in the stasis tube subsided. Norahc's head fell forward and hit the glass enclosure. He waited for the signal, then opened his eyes.

Bruce stood on the other side of the glass, his eyes red. Bloody tears streamed down his cheeks. He shook, though probably not from the cold.

Norahc pointed to the access panel and waited for the glass to slide open.

"What the hell was that?" Bruce screamed.

Norahc stepped out into the holding bay. He smiled at Bruce and turned toward the door. "I guess I forgot to tell you to keep your eyes off Gateway."

Bruce let loose a guttural laugh followed by a cough and few spots of blood. "Did you also forget to tell me where we were going? Did that slip your mind as well?"

Norahc stopped at the doorway and turned around. "No. I told you—three times, in fact. You just wouldn't accept it."

"That was Hell!"

"Yes. It even works as a metaphor, doesn't it?"

Norahc looked down the row of empty stasis tubes. "Time to go pick up another load."

Benjamin X. Wretlind *ran with scissors when he was five. At ten, he wrestled the giant ape creatures of Seti Alpha Nine while nursing a bad case of the measles. At fifteen, he was awarded the Nobel Peace Prize for blowing stuff up. At twenty, he admitted that only the scissors thing was true. He is the author of* CASTLES: A FICTIONAL MEMOIR OF A GIRL WITH SCISSORS *and is working on another novel to be released in 2012. You can read his musings at* http://www.bxwretlind.com/.

THE GHASTLY BATH

by Dawn McCullough-White

A young man dressed in black crouched in an alley between two city houses. The coming dusk cast deep shadows in every corner. Rain pelted him.

Off in the distance he heard an argument between a mother and child. Thunder rumbled overhead.

Jules sat in the shadowy darkness, watching the window of Gilbert's house intently. There was a candle in the window of the one-room home, a dirty little picket fence surrounded the place, and the man apparently threw all of his garbage in the alley, because Jules was sitting atop a pile of it. He suspected the culprit had to be Gilbert, or his neighbors, a young couple who fought more than two people in love probably ever should. He'd been sitting there half the day, listening to them, beginning to smell like rotten eggs while he watched.

Someone snuffed the candle.

Jules smirked. He jumped down from his pile of trash and leapt easily over the fence. Glancing around, Jules saw that he was indeed alone, and with that he peered into the window that faced the alley.

Gilbert was shucking off his pants, getting ready for bed.

Jules pulled a dagger and a blackjack from his belt and crept up to the front door. It was unlocked. Without hesitation he walked right in.

The other man's eyes widened when he saw Jules in his black clothes, with the emblem of the assassin's guild, a red letter A, embroidered on the front of his cape. Water dripped all over the floor.

"Who—"

"Gilbert Marklegrove?" Jules hissed. Gilbert was an older man, a jailer and sometime executioner.

Gilbert turned suddenly to reach for a pistol but tripped on his way to the table and fell.

Jules stepped over to Gilbert, who was face down, struggling to free his feet from his pants, and cracked him in the back of the head with the blackjack, sending him reeling.

Gilbert lay on the floor, tangled in his pants and long

143

underwear…not exactly the fanciest vestments to greet death in.

Jules stabbed him in the back. Without explanation. Without whys or hows.

After he was certain Gilbert had stopped breathing, Jules wiped his blade on the man's blanket and tucked away his weapons.

He took a look out the window to see if anyone had heard the struggle, and he was in luck—no one around. That was certainly one nice thing about small towns like this; there were so few people, and most of them went to bed early. That's what he'd been counting on. Generally he hated being sent so far away from Lockenwood for some simple hit, but this had been easy enough, he thought, chuckling to himself. Still though, he might've come in through the front door, but he was not going to carry a dead body out the same way. The window facing the alley would probably be the safest bet.

"And now," he muttered, dragging the dead man to the window and gradually shoving him out. Gilbert got stuck about halfway through, and Jules contemplated cutting off some of the excess bulge so that he might fit, but after a minute or two of struggling, his victim dropped into the muck outside with an unceremonious *slosh* of mud.

Jules breathed a sigh of relief and slipped out the window himself, landing more gracefully beside the corpse.

The young man next door was dumping his garbage onto the refuse pile in the alleyway. Their eyes locked. He looked over at mud- and blood-streaked body and screamed.

Jules flung a dagger. It caught the man in the stomach but did not have the effect that the assassin was hoping for, and the young man staggered out into the street, screaming even louder now.

A guard, apparently out for a stroll when the neighbor went into histrionics, sprinted around the corner and spotted Jules carrying away Gilbert's body. Usually Jules had no problem getting into places, killing people, and getting away unnoticed—it was the way he'd made a living for years, and he was good at his job—but this time his employer, or whoever hired his employer, wanted the man's body brought back. Jules didn't know why, and was a bit miffed at that part of the order, and as the guard came running at him he wished they had just asked for the head.

"Dammit."

Jules panicked and hefted Gilbert, then tossed him over one

shoulder and nearly collapsed under the weight. He had planned on bribing the coachman, loading up the body and making his way out of Plunyport in comfort, as the coachmen were quite used to working with the Association. But apparently that was not going to happen tonight. No, tonight he was going to have to lug Gilbert to the stables on foot.

* * *

Two lanterns lit the stable—one on a peg beside the main door, the other illuminating the bay horse tethered in a dirt hall between the stalls and the boy who was fiddling with the cinch.

Jules dropped Gilbert's body to the ground and drew his dagger.

The child startled as the assassin ran toward him, brandishing the shining blade.

"Get out of here!" Jules pushed the boy roughly to the ground.

The lad scrambled to his feet, nearly knocking over the lantern, and raced out of the barn.

* * *

The horse proved difficult to control. It spun around outside the stable, and Jules caught sight of the sheriff and several of the locals running toward him. They were still on foot.

He kicked the gelding hard in the sides. This got its attention. It stopped spinning and picked a direction. At first it just leaped forward, but Jules kept kicking it and holding onto the reins with one hand, pulling them back too tightly and confusing the horse. With the other hand he gripped the saddle, straining to stay upright as the animal raced out of Plunyport and on toward Lockenwood and Wick's tower.

He just needed to get into Lockenwood, back to the tower that was the heart of the assassin's guild. He'd be safe then. Generally the guild was left alone, well protected by the crown. It was only because that stupid neighbor had actually seen him with the dead body, that's what everyone was so up in arms about—that and the fact Gilbert was the town jailer. Apparently they didn't like their citizens being assassinated, even if Jules was wearing the cape with the Association's emblem on the front.

No one was behind him now. For one moment he felt his worry ebbing away, and then he snatched a glimpse behind him as the horse galloped blindly through the dark and pounding rain. As he did, he glanced down and saw that Gilbert's body was sliding off the back of the horse, until just one hand remained visible, still tied to the back of the saddle.

The gelding's gait shifted, and when the dead body slapped the back of its legs, it sped up.

"Dammit." Jules pulled back on the reins.

The horse did not stop. It bucked, throwing Gilbert's body into the air for a brief moment, putting pressure on the saddle as it fell back down onto the horse's rear.

The horse bucked again and raced forward at a dizzying pace.

"Whoa!" Jules tugged harder, panicking.

The body was going to be so damaged by the time he got back to the tower that the man who wanted Gilbert dead wouldn't be able to recognize him, and Wick wouldn't get paid... and then Wick would be angry and he wouldn't get paid, either.

"Why does this always happen to me?" He jerked on the reins again.

The saddle lurched to the side. A moment later he was floating, facing the sky, gazing into the darkness, and then he landed hard, splashing in the mud.

Jules covered his head protectively, but the gelding was gone. He stood up and wiped the mud from his pants. His ribs felt bruised, his legs muscles strained.

The saddle and Gilbert's dead body lay on the muddy ground in a heap.

He pulled a stiletto from the top of his boot and cut the rope holding Gilbert's hand to the saddle.

He examined the body, although it was hard to make out much in the near-complete darkness. It was definitely wetter than it had been before being loaded onto the horse, and muddier after being dragged, and a bit mangled and skinless in some areas.

Jules pulled the body up into his arms, as if carrying a child. He wished this guy weighed something closer to a child's weight, but he didn't, and to make it even worse, it was *dead* weight. Hauling Gilbert back to Wick wasn't going to be fun. He'd probably be walking somewhere close to five miles.

The assassin set off in the direction he believed to be north. He needed to find the canal that ran past Wick's tower. It couldn't be too far; Plunyport was on the other side of the canal, and then due north was the Azez Sea.

He walked on, the rain continuing its assault. He was nearly blind in the middle of the night, listening for the sound of the canal, but all he heard was the constant thrum of rainfall. The path he'd been traveling turned into a quagmire that could suck the boots off of a man's feet. Then the water began to get deep. He was sloshing through what seemed to be the edge of the sea. He wasn't certain what he'd stumbled into.

Jules dropped the body with a splash and brushed the long, dark mop of his hair from his eyes.

How far had he walked? A mile? Maybe, maybe not—that corpse was damn heavy. But it *seemed* like it had been a mile, and he was soaked to the bone. His wet leather clothes were heavy and growing more and more uncomfortable with every step he took.

"This is ridiculous." He reached down, searching in the dark for Gilbert's body. Something appeared before him. He wasn't certain what he was seeing, something shining in a sliver of light. His hands found water as he knelt down, but no Gilbert. Jules reached out as far as he could without leaving the place he'd been when he set down the body, calling out, "Where are you?"

He splashed forward, feeling around for anything that resembled his mangled victim.

"Gilbert!" He took a few steps to the right. "Wick is going to kill me—" he muttered just before he slipped.

There was no ground beneath his feet. His face raked over a rocky embankment as he fell. He was pulled underwater, sucked down into a fierce undertow into pitch blackness, and then propelled forward. His body twirled end over end as he fought the current.

In a panic he swallowed dirty water. He slammed into something hard and rocky.

Jules resurfaced, gasping for breath and clawing the murky water. He was in the canal. He must've walked right over the edge and fallen in. And with the storm, the undertow was driving him north at a furious rate. The idea of the canal emptying out into the Azez Sea did not sit well with him. That was much deeper water, and he wasn't certain he'd have the strength to swim back to shore if the current took him there. He was going to have to gather his wits and get to one of the banks. That was his only chance.

Regaining his bearings, now feeling certain that he must be in the canal and moving steadily toward Lockenwood, he cried out for help. Unfortunately, he didn't see the tower, which sat right on the edge of the Avon. What he saw were objects on one side of him that he didn't recognize—tall silhouettes against a dark gray skyline as he was swept past, still gasping for breath, trying to control his spinning in the rough, rapid torrent.

"Help!" His voice faltered. He was knocked into something large and solid that seemed to be in motion under the water as well. His legs tangled up in it for a moment, and then he drifted past it. Jules didn't have time to think about how badly his leg had been twisted as he slammed up against a hard, flat surface and then pushed up into some sort of wooden furniture, maybe a desk. It pressed him up against a tall, heavy object that crushed against his body as the current forced him along.

Jules felt himself spiraling. Then the back of his head smacked into the sharp edge of a building.

He groaned, reached for his wounded skull, and felt the slick, smooth side of the desk pound his face into the building again.

Confused, the assassin slid down into the rushing water. For a moment he was nothing more than a leather-clad rag doll, limp and washed away by the current, his long, dark hair twisting and swimming about him like ink. He buffeted against boulders and gasped for breath, filling his lungs with the tide.

His eyes wide and panicked, he pushed off a large rock beneath him. Breaking the surface, he managed to cling to another desk or table that had been somehow swept into the canal.

In the darkness he could make out the shape of a heavy, square sort of structure. Every so often a stone peaked out of the wash. He began to realize that he hadn't fallen into the canal, and he hadn't gone past the Association tower. As a matter of fact, he wasn't going north at all. If he had been, he would've reached the sea by now. No. Somehow he must have slid into a ravine and gotten caught up in a flash flood.

The desk he'd been riding bashed into a sandstone peak and turned sideways, then it cracked open and a bloated white corpse slid out, once more knocking Jules under the waves.

The assassin tried to dislodge himself from the corpse, but the crook of its arm had become entangled with the hilt of the dagger on his belt, pulling him along under the water, deeper and deeper.

He unsheathed his dagger, freed himself from the body, and popped up to the surface once more. He slammed against a large structure. His face was sore and bleeding. Still fighting the current, he desperately grasped the wrought iron bars of the edifice's only visible window. His legs were being pulled in one direction as he clung to the bars and attempted to climb up.

A bouquet of dead flowers brushed against him and was swept away.

He glanced up at the sky. The rain beat down into his eyes. Lightning flashed, and for one brief moment he saw clearly the upturned wooden boxes that floated past him, as well as the construction he clung go.

A cemetery. He was drowning in a cemetery. Those weren't desks that he had been riding on the current, but coffins, the building he clung to a mausoleum. And then he saw, as lightning ripped open the sky overhead, the peaks of grave markers sticking out of the onrushing water. Stone shafts dotted his vision, and here and there were various wooden caskets, broken and leaking bodily fluids into the bath.

Jules scrambled to get a foothold in the tiny, false window of the tomb. His legs were like wet noodles, and they went out even as he forced them to continue to support his frame.

He slid back down the rough yet slick face of the tomb, gasping as a sharp pain shot up his leg. He fell back down into the water, trembling, clutching one iron bar possessively. The assassin now dangled by just that one hand, up to his mouth in the floodwaters again.

A dead woman's hair streamed across his face as her corpse brushed against him.

In a panic he tore at the hair, clumps coming off in his fingers, and then lost his grip on the mausoleum.

"No!"

He was swept along with the dead body that, to his horror, seemed to be enveloping him. Tendrils of hair were everywhere, long and black and in his eyes. He thought of Wick, of her long red hair, her porcelain skin, her blue eyes, her young, lithe body. He was going to die here in this flood, in this graveyard, somewhere outside of a backwater like Plunyport. This was supposed to have been a simple thing. An easy job. Kill some ridiculous jailer and get gone.

He spat out the noxious deluge and grabbed onto an obelisk, wrapping his arms and legs around it as if it were a parent he never wanted to lose. The dead woman was still draped around him. She was newly dead, no longer bloated but covered with slime.

For a moment it seemed that he would be able to hold on. He braced himself against the unending tide as it wore him down. He cursed the name *Gilbert Marklegrove.*

The dead thing still attached to him was becoming cumbersome. He needed to pry it off, lighten his load. He squeezed his eyes shut, willed himself to let go with one hand, wiped the hair off of his neck, and forced the head down into the water. Then he let go of the marker with his legs and was nearly pulled away by the current.

"Gods!" He grasped for the top of the obelisk again.

The corpse slipped off of him and sped away on the current.

Jules fought to pull his legs in, to wrap them back around the marker, but he just didn't have the strength.

Several panicked farm animals swept past him, tumbling against the headstones and coffins and disappearing into the darkness.

As lightning flashed again, he saw the demolished remnants of a barn coming toward him. The side smashed against the mausoleum, a portion of fence knocking into his hands, but he held tight. Then the barn's frame loomed overhead. It creaked as it crumpled against the menagerie of rocks, snapping and shifting and coming down on top of him.

The stone that he'd been holding for support broke off under the weight of the crumbling wood, and he was lost under the ghastly water once more. His body was spent. He was unable to save himself as his back smashed into a gravestone, and then his right arm broke when it collided with another. He spun, limp, sucking water into his lungs as he writhed in pain…slipping under…consumed by the darkness…his hair twisting in the void, tickling his face. He felt the life leaving him replaced by a strange sort of lightness, drawing him away from the pain.

He then shot out of the water and slid up onto the side of the barn with such violence that it revived him from near death. The barn wall rocked from side to side, and more and more debris piled up beside him. Jules lay in the confused mass atop the makeshift craft, face down, one broken arm useless and lying at an odd angle to one side, a pool of blood gathering under his head.

He wished for death. In that one moment he had tasted it, however briefly, the sweetness, the peace. More than anything he'd ever felt before, he wanted that again. But instead he was in agony, too weak to move, with garbage and dead things surrounding him.

As he lay there, half clothed and broken, he spied a corpse lying beside him, stark white in the lightning, with a mangled face and a rope tied around one wrist.

Dawn McCullough White *grew up in Rochester, NY, and is a keen observer of people. She spent her childhood listening to her father tell stories about history and ghosts. This left an indelible mark on her psyche. It is not such as surprise that, at the age of fourteen she penned her first novel and has never looked back since. Dawn currently has a Dark Fantasy series out—*The Trilogy of Shadows—*available in Kindle and Nook and in print through Amazon. In her spare time she enjoys watching documentaries and keeping EA in business by buying up every single Sims expansion she can get her hands on.*

Facebook Fanpage: http://www.facebook.com/pages/Dawn-McCullough-White/125763474137312

Website: http://dawnmccullough-white.com/

WORLDWIDE EVENT

by David Dalglish

Jake Finley was sitting at his computer at 2:37 a.m. when the Worldwide Event struck. He started in his chair, not by any physical sensation but by the sudden lack of it. He stared at his monitor dumbfounded, his forum post momentarily halted. He scratched the stubble on his cheeks.

"The hell?" he said.

He pushed back his chair and stood, most of his weight on his left leg. Taking a deep breath, he kicked out with his right leg. No pain. No stiffness.

"What the hell?"

On went the lights with a flick of his finger. It was as if he needed to see, to know for sure he wasn't asleep or hallucinating or dead. He looked at his knee, saw the scar across the bottom of his kneecap. After the surgery, he'd had no cartilage left in the joint. At least he thought he didn't, but now, well...

He snap-kicked again, feeling like a short-haired, overweight version of a Rockette. No pain at all.

"What the *hell?*"

After a few minutes of walking, jumping, kicking and stomping like an infant discovering his feet could make noises, he picked up the phone. He had a terrible urge to call a friend, but he didn't have any. The closest person to a friend he knew was a paralytic man named Reuben who lived several hours away in Kansas City. And of course there was the whole middle of the night thing. He backed up his browser and hit refresh, scanning the titles of forum posts that had erupted over the past few minutes.

I might be crazy but...
Miracle?
Anyone else feel that?
God is here!

The words gave him the courage. He dialed the number.

"Hello?" Reuben's gruff voice said before Jake even heard the phone ring. It was as if Reuben had been waiting for him.

"Sorry if I woke you up," Jake said, staring at his monitor. He felt so stupid, so silly, but at the same time so goddamn happy that

153

he had to keep going. "It's just...well, you know my knee, right?"

"Jake," Reuben said, not even giving him the chance. "I'm standing right now. As I'm talking to you. Standing on my own fucking two feet, not a wheelchair in sight. Your knee's working, isn't it?"

"Brand-spanking new."

"I'll be honest with you," Reuben said. A bit of a chuckle came through the receiver. "I didn't know who to call. I almost called you, but I didn't think you'd believe me. You do believe me, right?"

Snap-kick.

"Damn right I do," Jake said, and he laughed and laughed.

* * *

click

"...eaves just two roses left: Greg and..."

click

"...with a final score of twenty-three to..."

click

"...still receiving calls, but it appears that this is not a localized phenomenon. We have confirmed cases from Canada, Mexico, Great Britain, as well as reports ranging from Brazil to Germany to China. I want to stress that, no matter how outlandish this appears, this is no jo..."

click

"...and who now can deny the coming of the Rapture? God's hand has come down and touched us all, and if these miracles do not affirm the reality of..."

click

"Whooooooooooooo lives in a pineapple under the..."

click

* * *

The next morning Jake went for a walk, because he could. He wore gray slacks and his nicest shirt, usually reserved for graduations, birthdays, and the occasional Sunday service with his mother before she passed away. Going outside felt like an event. There would be people out there, hundreds of them. The television had confirmed this. It all wasn't in his head, and it wasn't just him.

He stepped outside and onto the sidewalk. Doing his best to fight his tendency to limp, he picked a direction and walked.

Strangers smiled at him. Some held their arms, or winked, or clutched their stomachs with their fingers. It was like everyone wanted to tell everyone what it was that had been cured. Several men walked past carrying canes high above the ground, and Jake smiled with a sense of kinship at their quick, exaggerated steps. The whole while, he ached to talk with someone, anyone, but he knew them not, and they did not know him. So he accepted their smiles, their understanding, and let his ears steal bits of conversations between strangers, indulging in their closeness.

"For over fifteen years I've had rheumatoid arthritis in both my hands. Could always tell you when the weather's about to change. Now all I feel like doing is knitting..."

"Doctor told me just last week I had cancer. Can you believe it? Still got my hair, praise God, it's almost like he did this just for me."

"Now I'm not a religious man. I go by what I see, what I touch. Smart, you know? Now I wake up, not a bit of a cough, and you ask me who I think did it?"

At this Jake laughed and turned around. He wanted to appear happy, and he really was happy, but without anyone to share, anyone to talk to, he felt aimless. All his joy, funneled nowhere, building up inside and spilling into nothingness. Before he went back in his house he checked the mail. Flipping the envelopes through his fingers, he found his disability check. He ripped it open, a weird grin spread across his face, and with the flourish of a child opening a Christmas present he tore the check into pieces, tore those pieces into pieces, and then hurled them into the air. He watched the wind take them, scatter them across the grass and sidewalk like confetti.

"I need to go to church," he decided.

Ever since his mother's funeral he had not stepped inside a church. He felt like a burglar. His mind kept shrieking at him *it's Thursday!* Still, Jake's gut told him the small Baptist church would be packed, and he was right. He pushed through the crowd gathered at the doors, no easy task given his large girth. His slicked back hair and shaved face didn't feel like his own. Jake was terrified someone would notice him, ask how he was doing and how long it'd been since he'd attended service. The sluggish crowd made their way through the corridor to the pews. No one noticed him, and for some reason Jake felt disappointed. A wayward son like he, weren't there supposed to be trumpets, fanfare, and a father running down the road to greet his prodigal son?

Instead he found a giant room filled with people but no air. He struggled for every breath. A man in a black suit and white tie held a microphone to his lips and shouted hallelujah. Jake did not respond in kind, feeling embarrassed to reveal such emotion. There were no seats, so he stayed in the back, where the murmuring was strong. So many stories. Everyone had one. A disease cured. A pain removed. One single, prominent problem of their life…gone.

The church's choir picked up their microphones. The pastor in the white tie smiled and let them take their turn. Everything about them was spontaneous and jubilant. Jake listened, the joyous lyrics washing over him. He mouthed along, still not having the courage to sing. The first song ended, and then they began Amazing Grace. Jake had heard it sung many times before, a slow, lumbering song weighted by the burden of forgiveness, always somber, always mourning. Not this time. The joy in it floored him. He rubbed his knee with one hand, and his other he raised to the sky. He didn't care if anyone saw. There were a million hands raised high in that room, and he wanted to be one of them.

In that far back corner of that small Baptist church, Jake dared sing aloud.

* * *

The television was already on and waiting for Jake when he got back from service. Along the bottom ran updates about what had been dubbed *The Worldwide Event*.

"Even now we are receiving additional hard information," a pretty blond said, her makeup barely covering the dark circles under her eyes. "Hospitals all across the U.S. are reporting spontaneously healed trauma cases, gunshot wounds, but the most prominent has to be the cancer patients. We go now to field correspondent Alan Green."

"Thank you, Susan." Alan was a white man with brown hair and an enormous nose. Briefly Jake wondered how he had ever been allowed on television.

"Standing with me are lines of men and women waiting to be screened here at Sacred Memorial Hospital. All had been diagnosed with cancer sometime before The Worldwide Event, with many having already undergone months of chemotherapy. Ma'am, please tell me, why are you here?"

He leaned the microphone toward a pretty woman with a very obvious wig.

"Well my father's elbow has kept him from golfing for years, but now he's out swinging, but I can't go golfing to show my breast cancer's gone. I want, and I think we all want this, to prove what we already know. Our cancer's gone."

At these words the rest in line, which had shushed to listen to the interview, let out a loud cheer.

"Nothing but optimism here," Alan said, turning back to the camera. "And that optimism is well-founded. Every time someone leaves the hospital they've shouted their diagnosis to the crowd, and it's always the same: no cancer. Susan."

"Thank you, Alan," Susan said, taking the top piece of paper before her and cycling it to the back, as if it were relevant to her ability to read from the teleprompter. "I don't think this should surprise anyone, but church attendance in the nation has skyrocketed. Churches are reporting triple and quadruple attendance, with many holding additional days of service to accommodate the sudden..."

Jake turned off the television and sat down at his computer. He stared at it, unsure of what to do. For years he had hunched over his keyboard, doing his talking and socializing through games, forums, and voice-chat. Now he could walk. Now he could get out. But what was out there for him? He loaded up one of his favorite hangouts, clicked to start a new thread.

"I think I found God today," he wrote. "Now what do I do with him?"

After a few minutes he closed the browser, having never posted his question.

* * *

For the next two days he took long walks, wishing he didn't sweat so much and breathe so hard when he did. Sometimes he recognized a face, and he smiled at them when he did. Still no one talked to him, other than a courtesy hello or good morning. Sometimes he caught a few strange looks, and he had the feeling these people thought all the fat on his arms and legs should have been what was cured.

On Sunday he woke up, showered, and pondered over possibilities of work. He had been a lowly delivery driver when he'd blown out his knee. Hardly an exotic job, but what else did he know? As he slid the curtain away and stepped out, his heart halted. A twinge of pain tickled its way up his leg. He took his weight off it, clutching the towel rack hard enough to make it quiver. Slowly, gently, he put his leg back down. Again, a tiny tingle of pain. Jake let out a breath. He'd walked how many miles the past few days? Hell, his *good* leg hurt, too, now that he thought about it. Chuckling away his doubt, he grabbed a towel.

* * *

Jake decided to go to the park, hoping the trees and grass would help settle his unease. That feeling of aimlessness had grown stronger. There was something he should be doing, he knew, but he didn't know what. So he walked. In the park he saw a trio of women talking at a bench. Longing to join in, he leaned against a nearby tree so he could listen.

"I think that just proves God's grace," the lady in the center said, her graying hair up in curls. "Even though we don't deserve it, He has given everyone a taste of what heaven will be like."

"I hardly needed the proof," said a redhead on the left. "Not after Johnny's car wreck. But it's good. I haven't felt like this in years. You really think the rapture is about to happen, like Pastor Rick said?"

"Sure hope it does," the center lady said. "With half the nation stuffed into church this week, we might have a chance of filling heaven's bleachers after all."

"This grace, though," said the lady on the right. "That's what this is. God's grace, even though we don't deserve it. That's what we offer the world, us Christians, God's amazing grace."

Jake wandered off. He didn't have a chance in joining that conversation. He wasn't sure what the rapture was supposed to be, and the only grace he knew was in the song, which still moved him to tears when he thought of it. As he walked a man called out to him, jostling him out of his trance.

"If you wouldn't mind," the man said, sitting cross-legged in the grass with a plastic bag open before him. A few dollars and some loose change held it down against the wind. The man's clothes were dirty, his hair long, and his teeth yellow, but his smile was kind and inviting. In his lap he held a sign that read Hungry and Homeless. Desperate for conversation, Jake drifted over when his natural instincts told him to smile and continue on. Without a clue what to say, he stood in front of the man. Thankfully, he was spared from silence. The homeless man was an expert at guiding awkward conversations.

"Things just never went right for me, you know?" he said. He scratched at his face, which was covered with an uneven growth of stubble. "Tried traveling across the states, did that for awhile, but man, I haven't had anything to eat in a day or two, and I'm really hungry."

Never asking, Jake realized. His hand was reaching into his pocket, and the man had not even asked.

"Things not picking up at all?" Jake dared ask. "Since, well, you know..."

"Since God touched us all?" said the man. "Better, sure. I was blind, but now I see, like Jesus himself spat on my eyes, but it don't do no good. People look at me like it's my fault now, as if the whole world's been fixed. Get a job, they say, like I got a phone for them to call me back on, or a return address so they don't throw it away the second my ass is gone. Should see the looks on their faces when I ask for work. Praise God, I can see, but I'm still hungry."

As he was talking the three women on the bench stood and tidied up their coats and skirts. The hungry man held up his sign. Two of the women completely ignored him as they passed, the third glanced over and frowned.

"You're right, grace is exactly what this world needs," the center one said, their conversation never halting. Jake watched them go, a hard rock in his stomach. He pulled out his wallet and dumped its contents into the stranger's plastic bag.

"God bless you," the man said, tears in his bloodshot eyes.

"Sure thing," Jake said, hurrying off as if he felt the whole world pointing at him and laughing. When he got home he kicked a hole in the wall, then stared at it red-faced and more embarrassed then ever in his life.

Pain twitched and grew in his knee.

In school Jake had read how all the watches in Hiroshima had stopped when the bomb went off, so among the bone and ash they knew the exact time Hell had hurled up a piece of itself to Earth. Well, The Worldwide Event was that bomb, and Jake felt like the watch, stuck in place without hope of fixing. It seemed irrelevant that the bomb had repaired his knee. If a second bomb had fallen after the first, sucking up the ash and rebuilding the walls and giving life back to those who'd been vaporized, they still would have stood around dumbfounded and in shock. How does one continue on with living and working and fucking and dying after something like *that?*

Jake sat on his bed, head in hands. Depression, that roaring lion, was breathing down his neck, its weight heavy on his shoulders. In front of him was a shoe box. Inside that shoe box was a gun. Reuben had arranged for him to have it during his lone trip from Kansas City to meet Jake.

"You're one of us now," Reuben had said, handing over the gun like it was an initiation. "Don't let anyone tell you what life is and what it isn't. You know your life, you know what you have and what you live for. Don't you dare hesitate for fear of what those other faggots might say. You got that? Your life. You control it, and you can end it when you damn well please. Just keep the safety on at all times, all right? Last thing I need on my conscience is you accidentally blowing your fucking nuts off."

Jake didn't dare take the lid off the box. Seeing the gun, clean, black and well-oiled, might give him some crazy ideas.

To his right the television ran on mute. On the scrolling newsreel, the constant updates ticked across.

Scattered reports across the U.S. suggest symptoms removed during The Worldwide Event have begun returning in select individuals.

Jake tried to stand, grimaced, and sat back down. He cried.

* * *

click

"...think the most logical explanation is a global mass hysteria, except instead of a disease or fear it was a *cure* that spontaneously spread, perhaps building through increased..."

click

"...have sent nano-technology into our atmosphere from their spacecraft. Now listen to me, the sudden activation would have given everyone relief at approximately the same time, would have defied detection by our current medical professionals, and now perhaps they have run their course, or encountered problems with our genetic code compared to theirs, and then shut down."

"So what you're saying is aliens might be the cause of this Worldwide Event?"

"Well, that's one possible source of the nano-..."

click

"God's wrath has come upon us now! Woe unto you, Jeruselam, for in your disbelief Jehovah has revoked the gift given to us, and unless we embrace, *fully* embrace the blood of Jesus Christ we will burn in the fire that approaches, for the bible is clear, the afflictions we suffer shall only become worse! Pray for those you love! Beg God for forgiveness, for these are the days of Revelation, and the lion and the lamb shall return carrying a sword..."

click

"...reports from hospitals have only increased what many experts now believe were only psychosomatic episodes, although no one has yet adequately explained the x-rays showing cancer remissions."

click

"...anyone truly doubt the awesome abilities of the mind? The world, in its sorrow, yearned for a cure, and as our souls connected in the ether, we made whole our physical shells..."

click

* * *

Jake hobbled to his mailbox, his teeth locked tight as he fought the natural impulse to limp with his right leg. He fumbled with the key, inserted it backward, then flipped it over. As he pulled out the lone envelope, he noticed its address and immediately opened the flap. Inside was a single sheet of paper, a form letter with a statement followed by a single question.

It read:

Department of Social Services has received a significant amount of reports involving incorrect status involving disabilities and illness. In order to better serve you, we are asking that you answer the following question truthfully. Please check one (1) of the following boxes that best describes you.

[ ] My illness/reason for disability has dramatically improved in recent days, and not returned.

[ ] My illness/reason for disability dramatically improved, but symptoms have returned.

[ ] I experienced no change in my physical/mental disability.

Once inside, Jake checked the third box, cut his tongue licking the return envelope, and then smashed a second hole in the wall.

* * *

On the drive to the church, Jake kept rubbing his eyes as if to pull himself out of a very deep sleep. He winced every time he hit a bump. There were two reasons. The first was the pain that flared up and down his leg from his bad knee. The second was that the lid to the shoe box next to him kept coming dangerously close to slipping off.

He turned his radio to a Christian music station, hoping to find a hymn or something to calm himself down. Instead he heard vaguely sanitized rock with love of women replaced with love of God. He felt the stone in his stomach turn. Turning into the parking lot of the church, he kept running insane thoughts through his head, hearing Reuben berating him again and again, calling him a weak pussy, cowardly and afraid of everything. In his mind, he could offer no rebuttal.

Inside the church there was room to breathe, and the jovial atmosphere of elation and celebration was gone. A dark cloud settled over the hallways, and worry leapt from the red carpet like fleas. He found a spot in the back and stood, eyes closed and hands open at his side. One time, for a brief moment, he had been touched by God, but it was too brief a touch. He had not grabbed on, had lost the opportunity to be led, and within the church he prayed for another chance, another touch, to be clutched in a hand wiser than his own and led down a path far better than the dismal, dark loneliness he feared.

Somber songs. A band leader that told everyone to keep faith with a smile on her face that did not match her voice. The preacher was soaked with sweat, and he held the bible aloft like a lightning rod. And then they sang Amazing Grace. Jake's heart leapt. The song began, and he hoped for a regression to the way things were. He even prayed for his knee to be healed, for that glimmer of hope to be restored in his chest.

But the song did not move him as it once did. He heard the human voices, heard their worry, their sorrow, their desperation and exhaustion. Where was the joy in defeat? Where was the worship to the heavens as the lions consumed them in arenas? He opened his eyes. Where the Hell was he? A brief whisper, something intimate yet foreign, brushed against his heart. When the pain flared in his knee, and his prayer remained denied, he dismissed the feeling, hardened his heart, and limped for the door. As he did the choir began another song, one that seemed sickly perverse given all their circumstances.

"He touched me," they sang. "Oh, he touched me, and I've never been the same."

Lie, he thought. Damn lie. They were the same, everyone the same, and that was the fucking problem.

He turned the key in the ignition with a shaking hand. The radio flared up with the engine, and breathing heavily, Jake stared into nowhere, his hands on the steering wheel, the car still in park. Going home meant giving in. It meant accepting a long, painful life. It meant living on the aid of others, of constant awareness of his loneliness and lack of friends. Could he endure that? So many times he had thought no, and only a sliver of hope kept him from opening that shoebox.

But what hope was left? God had touched the entire world, and in less than a week things were back to normal. All the sorrow, the heartache, the good and the bad and the rich and the poor and the weak and the strong, all living in loveless discord. The same. How could he believe things would get better when that very prayer had given him nothing?

The words of a song on the radio slowed, and the sudden tempo change plucked him out of his mental coffin.

"*Good won't show its ugly face,*" the verse began.

Jake turned the volume up, imagining the church he just left filled with such vile, ugly good.

"*Evil won't you take your place?*"

Was that the reason for the return of pain? A callous reminder that the world wasn't perfect?

"*Nothing ever changes...nothing ever changes...*"

The devil's inertia was too strong, and who was Jake to fight against it? What if...what if...

"...*by itself?*"

Jake turned off the car and removed the lid from the shoe box.

The clip had thirteen bullets. A sudden inspiration hitting him, he ejected the clip, removed one bullet, and then shoved the clip back in. He got out of the car. Gun in hand, he limped back into the House of God.

He would be an inspiration. He would be a source for change. Their arthritis, sores, and bad coughs would return, but his wounds, his bullets...they would remain. They would remain throughout the lives of every man, woman, and child in that small white building. Forget pathetic wounds like sight, breath, and touch. He would show them God's *true* power. Sorrow. Death. Horror. Loss.

Let God heal those wounds.

Then all would see.

Twelve disciples.

Twelve bullets.

One Judas.

David Dalglish *lives in Missouri with a wife that is way out of his league and a daughter who was obviously conceived of better stock than he offers. He is the author of nine books, all blatant ripoffs of World of Warcraft and Dragonlance. His dream is to one day be an accountant for a Vegas prostitution ring.*

Of all his books, his most popular to date are the three novels in the Shadowdance *series*—A Dance of Cloaks, A Dance of Blades, *and* A Dance of Death. *His other series include the tremendous* Paladins *series, possibly the best writing he's ever presented and* The Half-Orcs. *He also compiled and edited—as well as wrote many of the tales included within—the anthology* A Land of Ash. *To read more about David and how overrated he is, feel free to visit http://ddalglish.com.*

WORLDWIDE EVENT

CHORUS

Bonus Story by Robert J. Duperre

The howling began at sundown.

Abigail Browning sat up in bed and drew her legs to her chest. Her entire body ached from the day's hard labor, muscles and joints groaning each time she moved. She cocked her head and listened as a tingling sensation crept from feet to knees to chest to head. These noises weren't exactly unexpected—Mort Hollis, the gruff old man who'd sold her the farm earlier that day for thirty gold coins, had warned her about the ramshackle town of Westworth's savage nightly visitors and told her to make sure her doors were locked tight—but there was no way she could have anticipated the alarming rawness of the sound.

It started as a rumbling, drawn-out mewl that drifted through the cabin like the hum of a distant motor. Soon higher-pitched screeches joined in, echoing in the audible space above and below the originator. The sound wavered in tone, scaling up and down, creating an abstract, primal melody. The window shutters rattled with each variation in timbre. It almost seemed as if they were shaking in fear. Abigail felt the same way.

She glanced to the door, expecting it to swing open any second and a frightened toddler to sprint into the room. He would dive under her covers and wrap his quivering arms around her while she in turn wrapped her arms around him, the way she did any time the coyotes back east began their nightly song. She would then whisper into his ear that all would be fine, nothing could hurt him, she would always be there to protect him.

But that wasn't going to happen. Nathan was gone. The Incident saw to that. Tears streamed down Abigail's cheek as she saw his once-beautiful face swollen and bruised. She remembered touching his forehead and felt the coldness of his flesh once more. She hadn't cried as she held him then, covered in blood, cradling him in her arms and singing his favorite lullaby, pretending nothing had happened. She more than made up for that now. Her body quaked with guilt from the memory, from the guilt of not having been there to protect him from the bastard until it was too late, and she choked on her sobs. It felt like her sorrow would never end.

And still the howling continued. Even as she wiped her cheeks with the dirty towel from her nightstand it persisted, filling the air, becoming thicker, more resilient. Abigail swallowed the last of her sorrow and swung her feet off the bed. The slatted wood floor was cold, the air even colder, and she wrapped her arms around herself as she stood up and wandered to the window.

Pulling back the shutters, Abigail gazed through the open portal, across the expanse of dust and dirt. She saw her cattle out there under the fading red sky, still as death, as if they too were captivated by the alien sound. Behind them was her fence, a crumbling barrier built from the rotting trunks of the last trees that grew in this barren part of the new world. And out there, beyond the cows and dirt and fence, rose the red clay cliffs, their rocky surfaces glimmering like blood in the day's final light. She saw nothing odd, no monster, human or otherwise, that could make the sound she heard. There was nothing but an endless expanse of sand and stone.

She thought she saw a shadow bolt across her periphery. Abigail slammed the shutters, locked them, tiptoed across the room, checked the safety bar across the front door of her shack, and then leapt back into bed. She rolled into a ball, sticking her head beneath the covers and breathing deep, trying to instill the warmth of her breath into the atmosphere inside her cocoon. It was cold at night, made even colder by the memory of her son and the strange, shrieking beasts outside.

Hours passed before it all ceased and she was able to fall into a restless sleep.

* * *

The midday sun blazed as Abigail walked along the boundary of her land, examining the livestock. Its glare turned her shadow into an image of Medusa, her kinky-curly hair transforming into a wig of snakes. Shaking off a shudder, she went back about her business.

The twenty heads of cattle wandering about had come with the farm, and though Mr. Hollis had promised they were of good stock, all she saw were sickly, mutated beasts. Some had missing or extra legs, some had too many or too few eyes, and all were slender to the point of starvation. Not exactly the perfect specimens, but she shrugged, assuming it would be hard to find better out here in the wastelands, especially considering there were still invisible pollutants lingering in the air that made plants whither and animals spit out teeth, bleed from their gums, and perish in the night.

She'd traveled out here in hopes of building a better life, a quiet existence far away from the crowds of frightened people back home; or at least that's what she told herself. In reality she was on the run from her pain and her guilt, from the knowledge that the one thing that defined her—motherhood—had been ripped away, leaving her empty inside. Over the last few months she'd pushed her body to the breaking point, traveling when she should have rested her tired bones, withholding nourishment when she should have eaten, staying out in the day when she should have sought shelter from the sun. She lifted her arm and gazed at the hands that emerged from her long, tattered shirt. Her skin had been dark to begin with, but now it was reaching the point of blackness. There were blisters on her feet and fingers, and she had frequent, massive headaches. Sometimes she wondered why she pushed herself so hard, but that line of questioning was nothing but a cover for the truth.

Abigail Browning was torturing herself.

She approached one of her disfigured cattle, a female with an extra withered leg protruding from its hindquarters. It stood apart from the others, facing away from her and releasing a strange, rumbling groan. The beast let out a snort as her fingers traced its bony spine. Its head shot to the rear suddenly and it kicked out with its hind legs. The superfluous leg flopped about and Abigail jumped back, barely avoiding a hoof in the face. She slung her rifle from behind her and shouldered it, just in case the frightened animal decided to charge. It didn't. Instead it trotted toward the others, who were gathered around the feed bins, feasting on a meager supply of grains.

Abigail stepped to the side as the cow left the scene and spotted the reason the creature had been acting so strangely. There was a calf there, lying on its side. It shivered as if cold, and a puddle of red expanded around it. Abigail moved closer, trying to see over its side, and froze. The poor creature wasn't moving on its own accord. There was another animal there, a tiny thing with gray, peeling skin, squatting in front of the calf with its head buried in its stomach. Its neck twitched back and forth, causing entrails to flow from the gaping wound in the calf's underbelly. Abigail slid back the bolt of her rifle, chambering a round.

"Hey!" she shouted.

The monstrosity pulled out of the calf, revealing a bulbous skull and a blood-soaked face that might have once been human. A pair of milky white eyes with tiny black dots for pupils stared at her. The creature had not a hair on its head and its grayish flesh was stretched and shredded. There was a hollow gap where the nose should've been. Its cheekbones were too wide, the jaw too narrow, and blood dripped from its frayed chin. It hunkered down, thin ropes of muscle tense, and then leaned forward and hissed. Abigail backed up a step.

The creature swayed from side to side before rising on its skinny legs. In a moment of panic Abigail almost squeezed the trigger, but she paused. There was something about the thing's posture that hypnotized her. It was no bigger than Nathan had been when he died, and the way it scrunched up its empty nose cavity, exposing its sharp yet gapped teeth, reminded her of the expression that came over her son's face whenever he tasted something that didn't agree with him. Her breath hitched and she lowered the rifle. The creature's shoulders sagged as it stared at her. Its head tilted, with one nub of an ear almost touching its bony shoulder, while virtually nonexistent lips puffed out, making it appear strangely innocent.

Abigail slung the rifle back over her shoulder and stepped forward, wondering why Mort Hollis had never mentioned the presence of these odd beasts. Her old leather moccasins sunk into the blood-drenched dirt. When the liquid swished beneath her feet, the tiny monster bared its jagged, dagger-like teeth and crouched into a defensive position.

"It's okay," she said. "You don't have to be afraid."

She leaned over the calf and reached her hand toward the thing, waggling her fingers to let it know all was okay. She didn't know why she did this. The creature had just mutilated one of her cattle. It was a monstrosity. And yet her heart pattered while she stared at it, and somewhere deep down she knew the tiny thing wouldn't hurt her.

"Take my hand."

The creature hissed one final time, spun around, and took off. It was fast—faster than a horse, from her perspective—and it cleared the fence in one leap. In a matter of moments it was but a speck on the horizon, rushing up and over the red clay cliffs until it disappeared from sight.

Abigail frowned, staring at the landscape. She wondered how the peculiar little thing survived being out there, all alone in the desert. Strange as it sounded in her own head, she wished it well.

With a sigh she shrugged the rifle off her shoulder, placed it on the ground, and knelt before the dead calf to inspect the damage. She ran her hand over its weathered hide, feeling bumps beneath the flesh, tumors that would've one day sprouted extra hooves or tails or whatnot had the poor beast lived. She purposefully kept her eyes away from its gashed stomach. It's not that she was weak in the presence of blood; she just didn't want to think of that strange little beast as anything vile.

When she reached the calf's neck she paused. There she found a festering sore, black and white and red, dripping pus. Lines of infection ran from the wound to its chest, along its sides and across its split belly. She sniffed and smelled the distinct tang of rot.

The calf must have died in the night, which meant her monster—and that's how she thought of it, as *hers*—was simply scavenging a carcass. Abigail smiled.

* * *

That evening the chorus of howls emerged yet again. Abigail once more tried to block them out, but the wails were louder this time, more insistent, more *present*. She covered her ears. It didn't work. So instead she thought about the odd little creature she'd seen earlier that day, praying it would be safe from the beasts that cried out in the night.

* * *

"So how's the old Batchell place?" asked the toothless old woman behind the counter.

Abigail raised her tired eyes. "Fine," she said. "Not getting much sleep, though."

The old woman nodded. "The Howlers keeping you up at night, eh?"

"Yes."

171

"That'll happen." Her crinkled hands tied a knot in the bag of feed Abigail had just purchased and handed it over to her. "That'll be seven silver."

"How about four silver and ten copper?"

"Fine."

Abigail dug through her satchel and removed her coin purse. After dropping the last of her money into the old woman's hands, she asked, "What *are* the Howlers, anyway?"

The woman shrugged. "Don't know. Some folks say they're wolves, but bigger'n the ones you see in books. The Sickness changed 'em, they say. Made 'em huge, gave 'em a taste for human blood. They been wandering the borders since this place was repopulated four years ago, killing livestock. Not many folks've seen 'em and lived, but those that have swear they're giant demons that'll haunt them 'till the day they die."

Abigail's eyes widened. "That so? Who was the last one to see them?"

The old woman laughed. "Ernest Batchell, actually. Left town soon after. Said they were stalking his farm." Her beady eyes narrowed. "Guess that'd be *your* farm, now."

"Oh."

"Ah, don't worry none." She placed her calloused hand on Abigail's. "You'll be fine. Old Ernest was batshit crazy, that's what he was. But maybe you should go get yourself a man. That'd help matters, wouldn't it? A man to protect you at night?"

Abigail grabbed the bag of feed, threw it over her shoulder, spun around, and exited the shop without the courtesy of answering her.

She grabbed her mule by its bit and led the animal through what passed for Westworth's town center—a collection of dilapidated barns and sheds with hand-painted signs propped against their dry and dusty walls. There were few people out and about, but those who did brave the heat of late morning cast her suspicious glances from beneath their hats. Eyes stared at her like spotlights from the center of soiled faces. All were male, and there was an aura of danger about each of them. A shiver ran up her spine.

But maybe you should get yourself a man.

No. Wasn't going to happen. Abigail didn't trust men. Not anymore.

CHORUS

* * *

Abigail marched down the road. Draped over the mule lagging behind her were the butchered remains of one of her cattle. It had taken her nearly two weeks to build up the nerve to slaughter the poor thing, but her feed bins were running low, as were her supplies. She needed to trade the meat in. Old Man Hollis had promised that a properly butchered cow would fetch a pretty penny in the town proper, whether the meat was low-grade and diseased or not. She hoped he was right.

The sounds of people shouting came to her from over the dune to her right. In her state of exhaustion—the damn Howlers seemed to get louder and louder every night, keeping her awake and scared—she assumed it was her head playing tricks on her. But then it came again, a human bellow followed by what sounded like the screeching of a cat. She looked around, her heart picking up pace. She was near the Mullin farm, the only other cattle wrangler in town. The Mullins were comprised of three brothers and their father, who ran the farm. She'd met them all once, at the market, and didn't walk away impressed. She was about to ignore it, but then the sound came again, and this time she made out a loud *thwacking* noise. *Just ignore it*, her better judgment warned her. *Keep on walking.*

Abigail didn't listen.

Grabbing her rifle from its pouch on the mule's saddlebag, she stormed across the sand, kicking up clouds of dust. The screams came once more, then again. She heard three distinct, frantic voices, other than whatever animal was screeching. Probably the brothers. Probably in trouble.

As she crested the hill, Abigail realized she was wrong. The Mullin brothers weren't in trouble. The three boys stood in a triangular formation, each holding a plank of wood. They took turns raising the planks over their heads, bringing them down hard as they could on whatever lay between them.

She inched closer, and her mouth dropped open. In the center of the human triangle, crouching and bawling, with its arms raised over its head while blood poured from the wounds covering its body, was her monster. It squealed in pain as another plank smacked against it, drawing a cut across the back of its hand.

Rage filled her. She raised her rifle to the sky and fired off a single shot. In the aftermath, all movement ceased.

The three Mullin boys stared at her as she trudged down the rise. They kept passing suspicious glances back and forth. She stopped a few feet away and pointed the barrel at them.

David Mullin, the oldest boy, probably in his mid-twenties, grinned. Most of his teeth were missing and his gums bled, obvious signs of Sickness. "Well what we got here?" he said, his voice cackling. "How're you, pretty lady?"

Abigail didn't reply. She shrugged her rifle to the side instead, letting it speak for her. The boys complied, moving away from the poor, wailing creature.

"Aw, someone's got a soft spot for the freak," said Barry, the youngest.

"Shut your mouth before I put a hole through it," snapped Abigail. He obeyed.

When the boys were far enough away, she approached her tiny monster. It shivered while it lay crumpled in a ball, but at least it'd stopped screaming. It rolled over and raised its white eyes to her. The mirage of a grin formed on its thin, frayed lips. Streaks ran down its cheeks. The beast had been crying.

"It's okay now," Abigail whispered.

"Like hell it is."

A shadow flashed behind her and she was knocked sideways. Her elbow struck hard sand when she fell, causing pain to flash up her forearm. Billy Mullin, the middle brother, ran past her, weapon in hand. The vulnerable creature yelped, its eyes bulging, as Billy brought the plank down once more, this time hitting it square in the face. A couple of sharp teeth flew from the thing's mouth, accompanied by a stream of blood.

Billy swiveled his head and stared at her, his expression gripped with rage. "This thing killed one of our horses!" he screamed. "And we ain't gonna take that from some mutie!"

Abigail's eyes shifted from Billy to the creature and back again. In her mind she saw Mitchell standing over her dead son, a look of perverse satisfaction painted on his face. She gritted her teeth, squeezed the shaft of her gun as her own rage took over, and rose to her feet. Billy's expression went from royally pissed off to rather concerned as she stumbled to get her footing and then charged full-bore at him, leading with the butt of her rifle. He must not have expected her to carry through with the assault, for he simply stood there, gawking. The ass end of the rifle slammed into his nose, and she heard an audible crack as the cartilage smashed. Billy careened away from her, wailing and holding his face. Blood seeped between his fingers.

She heard movement and spun around, swinging her rifle like a bat. Its stock caught David in the jaw. His head snapped back and he cried out in pain. Abigail bounced on her heels, holding the rifle upright, daring someone to make a move. The two injured boys stumbled about, not daring to approach her, while Barry stood as if frozen, his jaw hanging open.

Finally, Abigail swung the rifle around and shouldered it. She aimed it at each brother, one at a time, and said, "Now go away."

The boys turned tail, stumbling over the dune to their rear. David, holding his cheek (which was already purple and swelling), turned back to her. He spat a tooth out on the dirt and glared.

"Pa's gonna hear about this," he said, and then disappeared from sight.

Abigail stayed as she was, gun in hand, nerves on edge, for some time afterward. She feared the boys would circle around and attack her from behind, but after a while that worry evaporated. She threw the rifle over her shoulder and looked to the spot where the wounded creature lay.

It wasn't there.

Her head shot from side to side, but it was no use. She could see nothing but sand beneath a light blue horizon. Shrugging her shoulders and breathing deeply, she trudged back the way she came, hoping the mule hadn't taken off in her absence—especially since it still had a hundred pounds of valuable beef strapped to its back.

Abigail Browning shivered. She was sure she'd done a good thing. It wasn't right what they were doing to that poor little creature. *The Mullin boys got what was coming to them*, she thought. The beginnings of a grin spread across her chapped lips.

* * *

Evening came, and so did the howls. They pierced her eardrums with their shrill timbre, louder than ever. The dying sun cast glowing streaks across the ceiling of the shack as its rays slipped through the gaps in the shutters. She lit the candles on the table beside her, hugged her nightclothes tight, and slipped beneath her covers. Her hands were clenched and held close to her mouth. She sucked on her knuckles. That damn wailing sounded so *close* now, as if it was right outside her door. She shivered with terror, imagining the Howlers, whatever the beasts might be, barging in and devouring her whole. With that thought, she kissed away any chance of sleep she may have had.

Something hard smacked against the door, as if her fear had been given life. She shot up in bed and pulled the blanket to her chin. *Maybe it's nothing*, she thought, but then it came again, louder this time. The lone cupboard in the room shook with the impact, and one of her two drinking glasses fell over. It rolled across the shelf, dropped over the edge, and shattered.

All sounds—the howling outside, the banging at her door, the breaking glass—swirled inside her head. Her heart raced out of control and she screamed. It felt like she could have a heart attack any moment.

"Miss Browning!" a panicked voice yelled. "Miss Browning, they're after us! Help!"

Abigail cocked her head. She couldn't decide if the voice was real or in her head, but when it called her name again, followed by yet another loud bang, she jumped out of bed and sprinted to the door. There was someone out there. Someone in trouble, pursued by the Howlers. She had to help.

She gripped the bar across the door with both hands, yanked it from its moorings with a shrug, and tossed it aside. What followed was a prompt smack in the face as the door barged inward, sending her to her ass. She bit her tongue when she landed, and blood pooled in her mouth.

Her forehead ached, and something wet trickled into her eye. Her vision grew wobbly as she sat there on the dirty floor. She lifted her chin slowly, watching the door swing open and four sets of feet clad in filthy work boots tramp into the shack. Her eyes went from the boots, to the pants, to the tattered shirts, to four grim, scowling faces.

"Well well," said Ennis Mullin, his sons looming behind him. "This little lass the one who did ya?"

The three boys nodded; David with his jaw in a sling, Billy with his face wrapped in bandages stained red, Barry with his weasel-like nose scrunched up. All three glowered at her, hatred in their eyes. Ennis, however, simply looked amused.

"She's pretty."

With the front door left open, the howling ratcheted up a notch, drowning out the ringing in her head. Abigail tried to plant her feet and kick herself backward, but her heel found no purchase. Her vision wobbled and she felt close to passing out. She leaned over and dry-heaved, drool trickling from her bottom lip.

"What should we do with her, pops?" she heard one of the brothers ask.

Ennis, cocksure and sickening, replied, "Anything you like."

Hands on her. Beneath her armpits, under her knees, lifting her. The bed then beneath her, and a hard something striking her face. She collapsed, the back of her skull striking the headboard. She flailed her arms and legs as hard as she could, but the hands holding her were too strong. Then her nightclothes were tugged. She heard the fabric tear, felt the coldness of the open air on her bare flesh. Squeezing her eyes shut, she tried to focus on something, anything, to distract her from the here and now.

But all she could think of was the last man who'd seen her naked, Mitchell, and then of how she'd come home and found him on top of her son, holding a cord around his neck while Nathan's little face turned blue and his eyes bugged out, of how she'd grabbed an axe and buried it in the back of Mitchell's head.

She'd done so much—survived the War, then the Flood, then the Sickness—she'd brought life into the world, only to watch it get snuffed out by the man who'd promised to love and protect her.

Someone scratched her inner thigh. She came back to the real world, and that's when she noticed there was something missing. It took her a moment to realize it, but the howling had stopped.

Again something hard whacked her in the face, and blood cascaded down her nose. One of the brothers—she couldn't tell which, her vision was too hazy—grabbed her legs and tried to force them apart. She squeezed as tight as she could, but the pain seeping into her mind made her weak. Her knees buckled and shook, and whoever wedged his hand between them grunted. She wanted to scream, but nothing came out but a hoarse, wet gurgle.

Footsteps now, fast and plentiful. It sounded like a million ants crawling around her, their spiked feet clicking against the floor. Wood breaking, glass shattering, people shouting. She felt a withering sensation, as if she'd been transferred to another plane of existence entirely.

It took a great amount of effort, but Abigail raised her head and opened her eyes. What she saw defied description. There were bodies in motion everywhere—some dark, some light. There were men screaming and beasts growling, and every so often a geyser of red would erupt and strike the walls. Bones snapped, teeth gnashed, and still the screams of torment persisted. She felt as if she indeed *had* been taken away from the mortal coil, and now resided in Hell.

Something crept beside her on the bed, something large and glowing. A pair of cold, coarse hands touched her forehead. She glanced over at a muddled white oval with a torrent of red running down its bottom half. That was the last thing she saw before the blackness took her.

* * *

Abigail Browning lay with her knees drawn up to her chest. She was cold, so cold. She could've kicked herself for not starting a fire in the small stove that sat in the corner of her shack. It wasn't much, but at least it would've provided some warmth.

She reached down for her blankets, but they weren't there. She tried to move her head and was struck by a surge of pain that ran from the side of her face on down her neck. Her hand reached up and touched the sore spot. Her eye and cheek were swollen, and her nose felt like silly putty. With a groan, she opened her eyes.

There was no bed beneath her, only sand. And she was surrounded by sound—voices, quite a few of them, guttural and primitive, squealing. She gulped down the bile in her throat and raised her head.

All around her, creatures with gray skin sat cross-legged, their disfigured, horrendous faces aimed at the sky. They cried at the moon, their throats vibrating as the noises emerged. *I'm dreaming*, she thought.

Abigail gradually sat up, waited for her dizziness to subside, and then looked around once more. No dream. She glanced to her right and saw a female creature with gray, flapping breasts sitting beside her, eyes to the night sky. It acted like she wasn't there, and as its sunken jaw moved she saw droplets of blood drip from its chin and cascade down its belly, only to be licked up by the two smaller creatures it held in its lap. Abigail's eyes widened—really only the left one, since the other was virtually swollen shut—and one of the smaller beasts looked at her. There it was. The monster, *her* monster, the one she'd seen eating the dead calf, the one she'd saved from the Mullin brothers earlier that day.

The mother ceased her howling and her dotted black pupils turned Abigail's way. The female opened her arms, and the young one burst from her grasp, its malformed penis dangling. It barreled into Abigail, and for a moment she feared the thing would rip out her throat. It didn't. Instead it nuzzled its huge, bald cranium into her neck. Hesitantly, she brought up her hand and stroked its head.

The mother, apparently satisfied with the result, wrapped her arms around her remaining child and resumed her primal song.

Abigail sat there in amazement, holding the strange little life form. All around her she noticed it was the same scene, over and over again—female monstrosities with their young ones, weeping at the sky. She looked straight ahead, saw her farm in the distance, nothing but a speck, and gazed at the thing in her arms.

The child cooed, and then placed his crooked palm on her chest. That hand rose up and bony fingers wrapped around her jaw, moving it up and down.

In that moment Abigail understood the purpose behind the strange chorus. She mimicked the rest of the clan, gazing at the ugly yet precious thing in her arms while she sang.

"Hush little baby, don't say a word
Mama's gonna buy you a mocking bird
And if that mocking bird don't sing
Mama's gonna buy you a diamond ring."

The mutated child's eyes began to close, and a smile stretched across Abigail's face. After years of searching, she'd finally found a place to belong. She was home.

Chorus, *a story inspired by the illustration by* **Jesse David Young** *that accompanies it in this collection, originally appeared in* Dark Tomorrows: Second Edition, *a collection of short stories by* **J.L. Bryan**.

THE ONE THAT MATTERS

Bonus Story by Robert J. Duperre

Ash covered the landscape like cold, dead snow. Small lumps scattered throughout the yard, buried in the piles of blowing dust. They might have been objects forgotten during the rush to beat the easterly wind, the old feed buckets, or perhaps the remains of the chickens those buckets used to nourish. A cold wind blew, revealing a blackened joint. It might have been the elbow or knee of some poor soul who'd come in search of help; help they obviously no longer needed.

Guido grunted and turned away. Nothing he hadn't seen before. He continued around the old farmhouse, back creaking, lungs wheezing. Placing a hand on the back porch's stoop, he rested a moment. His eyes looked skyward. Dark clouds still loomed ominous overhead. They billowed deep and low, yet seemed to stretch for miles into the atmosphere. Water fell on the shield of his gas mask. He whisked the drops away with a wipe of his gloved hand, leaving trails of black soot. Another gust of wind caught him unawares, and he shivered at its biting cold.

Turning back to the task at hand, Guido circled his house until he found what he was looking for—a thick, curved metal construction that jutted from the foundation. He dipped beneath its lip, knelt in the mounds of wet, gray powder, and took a large brush from his belt. Originally used to clean the horses' hides, it had gained a new purpose, much like everything else since the eruption of the Yellowstone Caldera. He swept the bristles from side to side against the grate beneath the steel casing, clearing ash from the gaps in the filter. It was tough work, and his back ached with each stroke, but Guido Malfi was nothing if not a diligent man. Before long, he'd cleared the filter as best he was able. In another three days he'd have to come out again, but that was still three days he could spend inside, warmed under the cover of many blankets. Three days that he could spend with Her.

181

Guido slid the lock through its catch after he closed the bunker's overhead door. The sound of metal scratching against metal echoed through the small entryway, like fingernails over a chalkboard. He winced, waiting for the reverberations to cease. When they did, he moved to the second door and slid it open.

She was waiting for him. She sat on the couch, still wearing the *Bratz* pajamas she'd had on when she first arrived. Her brown hair was clumped and ratty, but to him, in the dim yellow light, it looked silky and beautiful. Her eyes lifted. She recoiled for a split second and then smiled. Her teeth were crooked, in bad need of braces she would never get.

He slid the gas mask from his head and took a deep breath. His lungs rattled, but that was okay. He'd lived with worse than that before.

The room was small, barely ten feet by ten, entombed by concrete walls four feet deep. This was Guido's pride and joy—a bomb shelter he'd constructed over the last twenty years, a bomb shelter folks assured him he'd never need. He chuckled. So much for them.

He'd stocked the cubby beneath the shelter with enough canned goods and water to last two years, though the girl had thrown off his initial estimations. Grabbing a flashlight, he lifted the hatch and looked inside. The gas generator that powered the lights and the air filter chugged along below the earth, its exhaust piped out to the surrounding woods. He smiled upon hearing its guttural purr. Snatching a couple cans of peaches from a shelf, he shut the hatchway and turned.

"Do you want some food, Alyssa?" he asked.

The little girl nodded.

"Yes please, Mr. Malfi," she replied.

They sat down to eat.

* * *

"Tell me one of your stories," said Alyssa. She picked up a syrupy peach with her bare hand and plunked it in her mouth.

Guido stroked his white beard. "Hm. Let's see. I told you about the Kennedy assassination, right?"

She nodded.

"How about G.W. and his plan to dominate the world economy by crashing planes into a couple buildings?"

Again, she nodded.

"How about the moon? Have I talked about that?"

"No," she said with a shake of the head. "Tell me that one."

"Okay. Well, it happened a long time ago, when I was a young'n in college. We and the Ruskies were always at each other's throats, trying to beat each other at everything, as if that would help distract us from knowing one side or the other would soon lose patience and launch the first nuke. One of the meanest competitions was this 'race to space' thing. Whoever landed on the moon would get some sort of bragging rights, take first place in this pissing contest we had going. So one day, we did it. We landed on the moon. The whole world stood up and cheered for us, as if we'd accomplished something. But here's the thing, Alyssa. We never did reach the moon. It was all a ruse. You know what a film studio is?"

She listened intently as he spoke, her chin resting on her fists. She stared at him with those wide eyes of hers, and he felt his heart melting. This little girl was everything to him, had been since the day she came running into his yard screaming while sirens blared in the background. The announcement had just come over the airways, and everyone was in a panic. Vandals tore through every corner of Mercy Hills, Connecticut, his hometown. The little girl had looked so scared, so on edge, when she arrived at the doorstep of his farmhouse while he was outside sealing the shelter from the rain of ash soon to come. At first he thought to ignore her, to turn her away like he had the Letts family when they came calling. He hesitated, though, and when he looked in those large, innocent eyes, he remembered the dreams of his youth, the love of his family. The family she'd most certainly lost in the chaos of a crumbling society.

So he'd brought her in. He'd saved her, and that memory filled him with pride. *Daughter*, he thought. *She is my daughter now. Or granddaughter, at least.*

When he finished his story, he smiled. They said their goodnights, climbed into their cots on either side of the room, turned off the lights, and fell asleep.

* * *

A sound awoke him. It was like static, or baseball cards fastened to the spokes of a bicycle. He sat up, his tired muscles aching, and searched for the pull chord in the dark. He found it dangling above him and yanked. The overhead light clicked on. It took a few moments for his eyes to adjust.

Alyssa was already awake. She sat on her cot, knees pulled to her chest. Her eyes, always wide, were even more so now. The poor girl looked petrified. The strange crackling sounded again.

"What is that?" he asked.

Alyssa clutched her knees tighter and buried her head between them.

Guido swung his legs over the side of the cot. The concrete floor was cold beneath his bare feet. The thought came to mind that there might be people outside, desperate people who would do anything, kill anybody, for a chance at survival. He grabbed his baseball bat from above his reading desk and went to the reinforced door. Pressing his ear to it, he listened. There was nothing at first, and then that fizz came again. Only it wasn't coming from beyond the door, he realized. It came from inside the shelter.

He glanced at his desk, walked to it, and sat down. Positioned on the side was his ancient radio, still plugged in. His fingers touched the volume and turned it up. At first there was nothing, and then it crackled. It sounded like static, but beneath, he swore he could hear a voice. He twisted the tuning knob—Guido Malfi believed in the solid construction of the old, and this radio hadn't failed him since his teen years—and slowly, the speaker on the other end broke into startling clarity.

"This is a message for all survivors," the voice said. It was male, polite, and had a thick accent. "My name is Colonel Martin Doucette. Citizens of the United States, we have arrived. We apologize for the delay, but we're here now, and we're here to help. As of this moment, our ships are docked and waiting for your arrival. You will be granted amnesty in France, if you choose to exit your homelands. We will remain docked for a period of one month, and hand out supplies to those that remain behind. The list of safe ports is as follows: Boston Harbor, Groton Harbor, New York Harbor..."

One hundred and twelve days of silence after the eruption, and it was the French, the goddamn *French*, who came to their aid. He couldn't help but smile.

THE ONE THAT MATTERS

They've always gotten a bad rap, he thought. *They may be a bit testy, but hey, they're French, so who could blame them? Americans seemed to have forgotten that if it weren't for them, we wouldn't have a country to call home in the first place...*

He wheeled around, snapped the radio off, and rushed to the aluminum chest that passed for a closet. Throwing it open, he tore through its contents. Clothes flew this way and that.

"What's going on?" asked Alyssa.

He turned, smiled, and started tossing articles of clothing at her. "These won't fit, but we'll make them," he said.

"We're leaving?" Her face brightened, almost wistful. He'd never seen her like this before, and it was the most gorgeous expression he'd ever laid eyes on. It was as if the months of isolation had been stripped away, revealing her as she truly was for the first time.

"Yes, Alyssa," he replied, his heart soaring. "It seems the cavalry finally arrived."

* * *

The cold outside was intense, the worst it'd been in weeks. Guido did his best to ignore it as he walked the first of many miles toward the harbor. Alyssa trudged beside him through the wet, mulched ash as they turned down what had once been Main Street. He didn't know what time it was, other than a vague sense of daylight. The dark clouds above, the ones that seemed to rush across the sky yet never get anywhere, were thick as ever. It cast an eerie gloom on the world. For a moment, Guido regretted their decision to leave. *We were safe in the shelter*, he thought. *Nothing could touch us there.* All he had to do was look down at his miniscule travel companion, see the expectant look in her eyes beneath her mask's Plexiglas, and those doubts faded.

Before long they reached the center of town. Most of the houses they passed had crumpled beneath the crushing weight of the ash. Windows were broken, leaf-barren trees felled, and cars overturned. Thankfully the ash covered all of these, hiding their atrocities, blanketing them into pale, gray lumps. That was okay by him.

The road signs were long gone, but that didn't matter. Guido knew where he was going. It was only three miles to the highway.

From there, a straight shot on 95 until they hit the connectors that led to Groton. On foot, it might take a few days, but he'd packed plenty of food in the sled he pulled behind him. They could camp out at night, or at least whenever it grew too dark to see. They just had to make sure not to breathe too deeply with their masks off.

They were almost out of the town boundary when they heard a loud whooping sound. Shadows darted in front of him, crossing from one wrecked house to another. More whoops. A rock skittered across the muck-covered pavement in front of them, scattering ash to the wind. Guido placed a hand on Alyssa's shoulder and pulled her in close.

Figures emerged from the shadows, five of them, hunched and swaying. They circled like a pack of wolves, yipping. Alyssa shivered against his leg.

The figures drew closer, and even in the bleak light he knew they were male, and young. They wore blood-drenched scarves over their faces, the color shocking against the stained gray of their skin. Their eyes danced with madness as they wielded planks of wood with nails driven through them. Guido held Alyssa tight and reached into the cart behind him. He pulled out his trusty Louisville Slugger and held it with one hand, ready to make like Mickey Mantle should the need arise.

"Don't come any closer!" he warned. His voice echoed inside his mask.

One of the men neared. He pulled the scarf from his face. Blood streamed from his nose and the corners of his mouth. His teeth were brown and rotting. He grinned, and it was sickening. He couldn't have been anything more than a teenager.

"We got no problems with you," he said in a gravely voice. "We just want the girl."

"Step away," Guido said. He held the bat high above his head like a lumberjack.

"We said you can go, old man," growled another before lunging forward. Guido lashed out with the bat, barely missing. His old muscles screamed on the backswing. The kid danced back and chortled.

Something hit his leg from behind. It buckled as pain tore into his buttocks. He dropped to one knee. It took all his effort to grab Alyssa before he fell on her. He pulled her against his chest and swung the bat wildly. He felt the wooden shaft connect. Someone howled in pain.

"Asshole!" one of the kids yelled.

Guido held his ground. He rose on his pain-seared leg and twirled around, thrusting the bat forward as he did. He caught sight of the wounded assailant, hunched on the ground, holding his head. He coughed. The remaining four closed in, encircling them. He knew he couldn't hold them off forever. At his age, it was just a matter of time.

"Listen to me!" Guido shouted. "There was a radio broadcast! The French have arrived! They have ships waiting in Groton, and all we have to do is get there. You don't have to fight me on this!"

One of the attackers—still wearing his bloody scarf—swung his board. It missed, and that only seemed to make him angrier. "Fucking liar," he grunted.

"I'm not lying!" bellowed Guido. Alyssa's head buried further into his chest. He felt her body quiver as she sobbed. Regret filled him. That light, that hope, he'd seen earlier was gone. Anger shook him to the bone.

The one who'd spoken first piped up again, this time in a softer, calmer tone.

"Listen, man. No need to make shit up. We know we don't got long to go. Just let us have some fun before then, 'kay? C'mon, you're a man. You understand. Right?"

Guido couldn't believe the words. He struggled with Alyssa's weight, his breathing coarse and painful. "You won't get her," he whispered. He didn't think they could hear him beneath his mask. He didn't care.

With a sudden fury, Guido charged. The surprised kid didn't move fast enough. The bat struck his head, which snapped sideways, streaming blood like a morbid sprinkler. His body twisted and then lay still as it hit the ground

Alyssa's weight slowed Guido's movements as the others attacked with a vengeance. One hit him in the shoulder. He hunched, protecting his precious girl with his own body. Another struck his thigh. He fell over, the pain horrendous. He rolled as to not crush the Alyssa, and then huddled over her. Someone ripped his mask off. Gasping, he inhaled handfuls of wet ash and began to choke. Another blow, this one on his back. He felt the nail punch through his clothes and pierce his flesh. It drove in so deep that when it retreated it felt like it dragged his insides with it.

The world turned hazy. Everything shook.

Keep her safe, his reeling mind insisted. *Protect the girl, save the only one that matters.*

Blows landed all over his body. Rusty nails drove into him. He grew weaker and weaker by the second. Alyssa clung to him as he fell to the side. He felt his blood leak out through the numerous new holes in his body, soaking his clothes and dribbling down his chin. And still, the girl clutched him.

A savage hovered above, tugging on Alyssa's hand like a fairy-tale beast. The girl screamed and kicked, not letting go. He tried harder, and that made her kick all the more. Finally he reared back and lifted the board above his head. The nail glinted in the faint light. Guido pulled Alyssa below him and closed his eyes.

A shot cracked the air. Another. Then shouting. They surrounded him, a chorus of chaotic voices. Guido held the girl, wishing he had a womb into which he could stuff her for protection. He was about to die, and even worse, so was she. In the only thing he'd cared about in a long, long time, he'd failed.

But there were no more blows. The shouts ceased, as well as the gunshots. Guido lay still, afraid to move. Alyssa squirmed in his arms. He could hear her breathing inside her mask. It sounded like a freight train.

Hands grabbed his mangled body. They rolled him over. He felt weak, and with blurred vision he watched a man lift Alyssa up. He held her out as if inspecting a sensitive work of art. Beside him was another human form, this one was smaller and holding a rifle. It kicked the motionless body at its feet. Several others walked by, just ghosts in his fogged eyesight. Their voices chattered on.

A shadow blocked out his vision. A man's face. He wore a bandana over his nose and mouth, blood soaked like the others. The eyes though...blue, kind, and concerned.

"My name's Jason," the man said. "We're friendly. Who were those kids?"

"Gone wild," Guido said, his voice rough and weak. "And hungry...hungry for things they shouldn't, they shouldn't..."

Jason glanced over at Alyssa and then nodded to show he understood.

"She's all right now?" he asked, unable to look for himself.

"She is," Jason said. "She's with my daughter, Melissa."

Guido tried to nod, but didn't have the energy.

"Did you hear the announcement?" he heard a young girl ask, most likely Melissa.

Alyssa responded, still quivering but on the edge of excitement. "We did."

"They've come!" said the girl between coughs. "We'll be safe and warm!"

Guido felt a bit of gratitude as Jason lifted his head so he could see her better.

"We'll take care of her for you," he whispered. "What's her name?"

"Alyssa," Guido coughed. "My granddaughter."

Contented, he leaned his head back, smiled, and let the darkness take him.

The One That Matters *originally appeared in the best-selling anthology,* A Land of Ash*, edited by* **David Dalglish**.

TRAIPSING THROUGH THE DARK
THE STORIES BEHIND THE STORIES

PLASTIC

J.L. Bryan: "Plastic" was written specifically for this anthology. Rob told me the theme was isolation, and this idea popped into my head—someone who's all alone but surrounded by every kind of consumer goods imaginable. The character creates/hallucinates a world where he is not alone, with bizarre and funny consequences. I think the strongest inspiration for this story actually came from one of Rob's stories in the first Gate anthology: "Sullivan Street." I wanted to explore something similar, a character with a life that was wealthy in a material sense but spiritually and emotionally empty. On top of that, it was great fun to figure out how an entire human life could be represented by different retailers at the mall. When I was a kid, I used to fantasize about living in a big shopping mall, probably after I read a book about kids who ran away from home to live in a museum. So, mix all those elements together, and you get the odd story of "Plastic."

THE INDIAN ROPE TRICK

D.P. Prior: Back in the summer of 2011 my son Theo got heavily into zombies. It started with *Marvel Zombies* and swiftly progressed to *Resident Evil*. It struck me at the time that I'd always studiously avoided the zombie genre and so felt it was about time I gave it a look. I started with George A. Romero's *Night of the Living Dead* and was surprised at how good it was. This led to *Dawn of the Dead* (including the excellent 2004 remake), *Day of the Dead*, *Survival of the Dead, Land of the Dead,* and Lucio Fulci's *Zombie Flesh Eaters*. By this stage it was a case of 'in for a penny, in for a pound', and so I watched as much of the genre as I could lay my hands on, some of it good, much of it exceedingly bad: *Quarantine, Quarantine 2, Zombieland, Shaun of the Dead, 28 Days Later, 28 Weeks Later, The Dead* ...

By the end of the summer, Theo was thoroughly sick of zombies and heavily into Nerf guns. It was about that time I wrote an article for the blog *Two Ends of the Pen* called 'Zombies on my Mind', which was my attempt at rationalizing the genre. That pretty much brought my zombie phase to a conclusion until Rob asked if I'd like to contribute to *The Gate 2*. Having read the first two books of Rob's *The Rift* series, which is steeped in zombies, I couldn't resist having a bash at the genre myself.

The Indian Rope Trick was a challenge to write in many ways. First off, I only had a couple of weeks to write it from start to finish due to the publishing deadline for *The Gate 2*. Next, and perhaps hardest, was attempting to write from a nine year old's point of view. There were also issues regarding the balance of comedy and horror, gratuity, and language that needed to be addressed.

The writing itself was thoroughly enjoyable, which is not always the case. It was a great opportunity to experiment with style, and I got to play around with speech rhythms, particularly when Wesley gets agitated.

NIGHT NIGHT

Daniel Pyle: As the eldest of five brothers, I was rarely alone as a child. In some ways, this was great—I usually had a playmate if I wanted one, and all those little bros made it much easier to gang up on our parents...Brussels sprouts for dinner? We don't think so—but there were times when I wished they'd all go away for a while so I could get a few measly minutes of peace and quiet. Think Home Alone. In Missouri. With a smaller house.

When Rob told me that one of the themes of this anthology was going to be isolation, I decided to play around with the idea of siblings and alone time. I wanted to write about older siblings. Maybe because my brothers and I are grown up now—or as grown up as we're ever going to get—or maybe because I didn't like the idea of killing off a kid on page one of my story (page three would have been fine). I also wanted to add a twist, which I won't give away here in case you're one of those weirdos who reads the notes before the stories. In the end, I was very happy with how it turned out. In fact, I think this might be my best story yet. It's my favorite anyway, and I hope you enjoyed it too.

DEAD THINGS

Michael Crane: This story started with an image in my head of an old woman knocking on her neighbor's door, screaming about zombies. I thought it'd be fun to have a character that clearly wasn't right in the head, although I knew that she wouldn't be the main character, nor would the story only be about her. It was just a starting point for me. I learned more about the characters as I continued to write, not exactly sure where it would all lead. That's when writing is the most exciting for me. When your characters take you on a journey where you're not sure how it'll all play out in the end.

DOES LAURA LIKE ELEPHANTS?

Steven Pirie: In *Does Laura like Elephants?*, I wanted to explore the relationships between four characters, two couples who had essentially been cheating on each other, with one of the characters, Laura, set in her own, distant, stroke-induced twilight world. This dysfunctional setup gave me a character who was there, yet at the same time was lost, and I wondered how that would add to the dynamics of the four of them. Laura could not speak or interact meaningfully, so I gave her an occult-like relationship both within herself and with Don, her lover. I was keen to inject humour, as I believe that's what folk would turn to for respite in such a situation. Of course, I have exaggerated it somewhat for effect. What emerged is a story that has hidden depths and is one of my favourites.

39 DAYS

Robert J. Duperre: The inspiration for 39 Days actually came from a short story I read a while back, *Sweepers* by Leslianne Wilder. It was a great—albeit very short—tale about rising oceans and people trapped in a skyscraper. Though I loved the story, I couldn't help but think the tale could have been stretched out, made more personal.

So when Dan Pyle contacted me hoping I could write a story for his *Unnatural Disasters* anthology, I took the same basic premise, changed it around to make it my own, and focused on the people involved instead of the events themselves. What came out on the other side is probably the best short story I've ever written...or at least my own personal favorite.

THE GATE 2: 13 TALES OF ISOLATION AND DESPAIR
THE CANDLE EATERS

K. Allen Wood: When I set out to write "The Candle Eaters," I wanted to do something with Halloween as the backdrop. I'd long had the idea for the story, and when another small-press magazine announced they were putting out a Halloween issue, I had the perfect reason to finally write it.

I had four months to get it done. Plenty of time. However, before I knew it, those four months had dwindled to just three weeks.

The first version I wrote was extremely dark, featured characters with few redeeming qualities, and had an ending full of death and destruction. This was not the story that had been in my head for so long.

With no time for a rewrite, I submitted it anyway—and was promptly rejected.

What I did accomplish with that first version, I think, was come up with some original elements within the well-worn Halloween setting. Specifically the "candle eaters," which of course are a riff on the old-time tradition of using hollowed-out turnips or pumpkins to ward off evil spirits.

When Rob e-mailed asking if I'd like to send him something for *The Gate 2*, I said I would. When he said the theme would be "isolation and despair," I immediately thought of this story.

On the surface, the story included here isn't drastically different from that first version, but after a few rewrites I think it accomplishes what I'd initially envisioned so long ago, which was a story fundamentally about faith and hope without being overly sentimental.

(I also managed to sneak in a reference to one of my favorite bands, The Dead Milkmen.)

Ultimately, I just hope "The Candle Eaters" is a good, entertaining story.

BLACK MARY

Mercedes M. Yardley: The invitation to this anthology came about at a particularly difficult time. My husband and I were delighted to discover that we were expecting triplets (surprise!) but ended up losing two of our little girls. The third is happy and healthy. Writing was a struggle and Robby D. and his artist, Jesse

Young, were kind enough to pitch a few ideas to help get my creative juices flowing. One idea was a girl who was alone on an island.

This struck me. A lonely girl seemed like such a beautiful thing to play with. I created a horrifying yet feasible scenario where a little girl was left alone except for the unwanted company of her abductor. The only other individual to talk to is a rather strange friend called Black Mary. The eventual arrival of the littlest Red Mary spurs the girl into action. Are the Marys figments of the girl's mind brought on by her abuse and isolation? Are they ghosts from the man's previous victims? That's not for me to tell you.

Perhaps her mind is creating companionship. Perhaps she is haunted. It would seem that I am haunted, as well.

EXHIBIT C

David McAfee: This is the third installment in my series of short stories dealing with a very talkative serial killer. The other two can be found in his two short story collections: The Lake and 17 Other Stories, and Devil Music and 18 Other Stories. Like the previous entries in the series, I hope Exhibit C is brutal, creepy, and disturbingly entertaining to those who read it.

THE CANOE

Joel Arnold: *The Canoe* started with a vision I had of a canoe that keeps appearing mysteriously at the dock of a cabin in the deep north woods of Minnesota no matter how many times the cabin's owner releases it back into the current of the river. I decided to have the characters be a father and son of Cambodian decent; the father living with memories of the terrors of Pol Pot's regime, while the son just wants to fit into American society. I peer-tutored Cambodian kids when I was in high school at a time when these kids still remembered living under Pol Pot's rule, and ever since then I have been fascinated by their stories of survival in such harsh and nightmarish conditions. But as *their* children who *didn't* experience that nightmare first-hand grow up in *American* society, those experiences are only stories their parents and grandparents may or may not tell them. And being kids, they often just want to fit in with their American peers. I wanted to write about this dynamic between father and son; how the father wants to protect his son, while the son just wants to find his own group of peers. While the canoe in the story at first serves as a way for the father and son to bond, it later becomes something that keeps the father and son apart.

On a side-note, the canoe has the name 'Farbanti' written on it, which—although not explained in the story—is in reference to a Norse god who ferried the dead to the underworld.

DESTINATION

Benjamin X. Wretlind: *Destination* was a concept piece. I wanted to write something in the science fiction genre, but being a horror writer at the time, I didn't know what to do. So, like most people, I borrowed an idea from something I had written a long, long time ago: THE FERRYMAN, a short story about Charon, the old guy who ferries souls across the River Styx but hates his job. That piece turned into DESTINATION nearly a decade and a half later.

THE GHASTLY BATH

Dawn McCullough-White: I was looking at some of the photos of damage that had been done to cemeteries in the aftermath of Hurricane Katrina—the flooding, the broken tombs—and then this idea came to me about a person caught up in a flash flood that tears through a cemetery, and how gruesome and horrifying that might be. And that was when I knew, this was my story, I wanted to put some poor sap into that situation. I also thought this would give me the chance to continue writing about Jules, an assassin and favorite character in my trilogy (the Trilogy of Shadows). Just explore a little bit more about his life prior to my books and I'd also have the chance to torture him a bit more...

WORLDWIDE EVENT

David Dalglish: Origins for Worldwide Event (originally titled Too Brief A Touch until mocking by other various authors in this collection prompted a change) are fairly simple. Shouldn't be too surprising that religion plays a part. It involved the question, if God existed, why didn't he simply announce himself to the world, removing all possible doubt? Ignoring arguments involving faith and belief being relevant should such a thing be a undisputable fact, my initial response was very simple: it just wouldn't matter. God could appear in the clouds, wave his hands, and go "Hi guys!" and there'd still be people out there claiming aliens, tainted water, group hallucinations, government conspiracies, etc. He'd have to appear again. And again. And again, like some goofy timeclock. "It's New Year's everybody, wave hi to God!"

But what if something did happen? What if, for just a brief moment, the whole world was made aware of something bigger than ourselves?

That idea, combined with one of my favorite Ray Bradbury short stories of all time, The Last Night of the World, became what was eventually titled Worldwide Event. It's a pretty dark story, but then again, I don't see how to make it end joyfully. If I ended it midway through, then it'd have been rainbows and sunshine without difficulty. But when exploring the possibility that the greatest miracle of our time would still not be enough to change *anything*...well...I consider that just a little dark. Just a little depressing. Never my intent, but rarely does my intent every really matter when I'm writing a story. The story's the boss, after all. I'm just along for the ride.

CHORUS

Robert J. Duperre: This tale was directly inspired by the fantastic illustration of Jesse's that graces the back cover of this book. When I first saw it, I immediately pictured a story of sadness and terror that also had a sort of beauty to it, a hope in the future that the horrible beings the image presented had no right to feel. When J.L. Bryan asked me to contribute a story to the re-release of his own short story collection, I decided enough was enough and finally put what was in my head on paper. Abigail's depressing story and eventual salvation is what came out. I'm quite happy with it.

THE ONE THAT MATTERS

Robert J. Duperre: At the beginning of last year, David Dalglish contacted me, wondering if I could possibly write up a story for him to include in *A Land of Ash*, a compilation dealing with the eruption of the Yellowstone Caldera and its aftermath.

Of any story I've written, this one was the hardest, both in execution and idea. I struggled for weeks to just come up with a plot. Every story I began ended less than a thousand words in, as it was plainly obvious that the story just wasn't working.

Finally, I took some of the conspiracies my father-in-law told me, imagined them coming from the mouth of an old man who'd prepared for circumstances much like this, and placed a young girl in his care. In the original version of the story, an important event in Guido's life, the event that made him shut himself off from society, is presented in between each break as a flashback. When I finished writing it, although I thought it was decent, my wife said it needed a lot of work and I agreed. I was ready to tell Dave forget it, that I couldn't get him anything in time, but he was stalwart. "Just send it to me," he said. "I'll see if I can find out what's making it seem stinky."

The next day Dave sent the story back to me, chopped almost in half. All of Guido's weighty backstory was eliminated, and what I read was a tightly knit, well-written tale of isolation and despair. In other words, this story wouldn't have been half as good as it is without Dave, and for that he deserves tons of thanks. It's one of the best pieces of fiction that has my name attached to it, it is the inspiration for the cover of this anthology, and has a feel and pace that I try to mimic each time I sit at my desk and plug away.

In other words, it's the perfect choice to close out this collection.

So that's it, folks. You've come to the end of our little journey through depression and loneliness. Please, if you liked this collection (or even if you hated it), feel free to stop by Amazon or whatever outlet you picked it up at and leave a review. Your opinion matters to us, as it should for every small press publisher. And also, make sure to visit http://theriftonline.com for updates on current and future projects from T.R.O. Publishing.

TRAIPSING THROUGH THE DARK

Look out for *The Gate 3: 13 Stories of Monsters Among Us*, slated to be released between November of 2012 and January of 2013. Trust me, it's going to be another good'un.

Robert Duperre
January 21st, 2012